Sabrina turned toward the door. "Just wait till I tell Aunt Hilda and Aunt Zelda about this. Just wait till I—"

Roland toddled around and threw himself between Sabrina and the door. "Sabrina. Wait. Believe me—"

"Forget it, pal. I'm—"

"Sabrina. Just look."

Something in Roland's voice made Sabrina stop. She let him lead her over to the full-length mirror that she had on her closet door.

And when she looked into the mirror—the mirror she used to check out her hair and clothes every morning before school—she couldn't believe her eyes.

There was nothing there.

Sabrina, the Teenage Witch® books

Available from ARCHWAY Paperbacks

Sabrina The Teenage Witch®

It's a Miserable Life!

Cathy East Dubowski

Based upon the characters in Archie Comics

**And based upon the television series
Sabrina, The Teenage Witch
Created for television by Nell Scovell
Developed for television by Jonathan Schmock**

AN ARCHWAY PAPERBACK
Published by POCKET BOOKS
New York   London   Toronto   Sydney   Singapore

This book is a work of fiction. Names, characters, places, and incidents are products of the author's imagination or are used fictitiously. Any resemblance to actual events or locales or persons, living or dead, is entirely coincidental.

AN ARCHWAY PAPERBACK *Original*

 An Archway Paperback published by
POCKET BOOKS, a division of Simon & Schuster, Inc.
1230 Avenue of the Americas, New York, NY 10020

Copyright © 2000 by Viacom Productions, Inc. All rights reserved.

All rights reserved, including the right to reproduce
this book or portions thereof in any form whatsoever.
For information address Pocket Books, 1230 Avenue
of the Americas, New York, NY 10020

ISBN: 0-671-04071-5

First Archway Paperback printing November 2000

10 9 8 7 6 5 4 3 2 1

AN ARCHWAY PAPERBACK and colophon are
registered trademarks of Simon & Schuster, Inc.

SABRINA THE TEENAGE WITCH and all related titles, logos,
and characters are trademarks of Archie Comics Publications, Inc.

Printed in the U.S.A.

IL 4+

It's a Miserable Life!

Chapter 1

☆

"Scrooge!"

Sabrina Spellman smacked a tray full of used latte cups on the counter at the coffee shop where she worked. She glared at her boss, Josh, her blue eyes flashing.

Josh set down the metal pitcher of milk he was steaming and frowned. "I beg your pardon?"

"Scrooge—you know, the guy in Charles Dickens's *A Christmas Carol?*"

"The dude who hates Christmas."

Sabrina nodded. "Yeah. Well, let me tell you, right now I think he got things right."

Josh laughed and poured the steamed milk into a huge coffee bowl half filled with strong coffee to make café au lait. "Come on, Sabrina. I never figured you for the Scrooge type. I thought you loved Christmas."

"Not this year," she answered. "At least not tonight."

Josh set the café au lait on a tray for Sabrina to serve. "What's wrong?"

"People!" Sabrina exclaimed. "Everybody at school is wired because the holidays are coming up. The customers we've had tonight—they're all rushed and tired and crabby. Complaining about all the shopping they've got left to do—and what the heck are they supposed to get for Aunt Gertrude. Complaining because the service here is too slow and they're in a rush. I mean, the whole point of a coffee shop is that it's a place to come to and relax."

"Yeah, I know." Josh shrugged. "The holidays are a busy time. People have a lot of extra stuff to do. Don't let it get you down."

Sabrina sighed. "I'll try."

Josh handed her the tray with the café au lait. "Who's this for?"

"Your favorite customer." Josh grinned and nodded his head toward the men's room door.

Harvey? Sabrina thought, cheering up immediately. But when she turned around with the tray, it wasn't her boyfriend she saw coming her way.

It was Scrooge himself—Mr. Willard Kraft, principal of Westbridge High School. Resident grouch. And—Sabrina hated to even think about it—her Aunt Zelda's current boyfriend.

"Sure you don't want to get this one?" Sabrina muttered.

Josh chuckled. "He's all yours."

"Thanks."

"Merry Christmas!" Josh whispered after her.

Sabrina shot him a look over her shoulder, then hurried over to her customer. "Hi, Mr. Kraft. Where's your table?"

Mr. Kraft didn't answer. He held his glasses by the wire frames and peered down at the tray as if he'd never seen a cup of coffee before.

"Uh, Mr. Kraft? . . ."

"Where's the cinnamon?" he demanded. "I specifically asked for a light sprinkle of cinnamon on my café au lait."

"Well, I—"

"Perhaps you should double-check your orders before you serve them, Miss Spellman."

"Yes, sir, but—"

"Maybe this lack of attention to detail is what tripped you up on this last history test."

Ten, nine, eight, seven . . .

Counting backward from ten was one of the tips Aunt Zelda had given to Sabrina when she felt like turning someone into a frog. *Or a pineapple. Or a snowman out in front of the store!*

3

Sabrina was a teenage witch. Well, half witch. Her father was a warlock and her mother was a mortal. For now she was living with two witches— her dad's sisters, Aunt Zelda and Aunt Hilda—who were teaching her how to use her powers.

Six, five, four . . . It's not working. . . .

"Well?" Mr. Kraft said.

"I'll get the cinnamon, sir," Sabrina said politely. *Three, two, one . . .*

"Where's the cinnamon?" Sabrina asked Josh through gritted teeth. "Ten, nine, eight . . ."

"Counting again, huh?" Josh laughed and handed her the metal shaker. He was familiar with the effect Mr. Kraft had on people. "Here you go. And remember," he teased, "the customer is *always* right."

Sabrina made a face, then headed back to Mr. Kraft's table.

He was sitting at a small table near the door. Just before Sabrina reached him, a crowd of kids from school swarmed in the door, laughing and joking and fooling around.

Sabrina moved over to avoid getting run into, then leaned down over Mr. Kraft to serve his coffee—

Just as one of the kids bumped her in the elbow, hard!

Oh, gosh! Please, no—

It was hard not to use one's powers to avert

a disaster. Especially when the disaster involved a large bowl of hot coffee and your principal.

But Sabrina had been schooled by her aunts to keep her powers secret at all times.

And so she watched helplessly as the hot coffee splattered all over Mr. Kraft.

"Look out!" the man shrieked and jumped to his feet as the hot coffee seemed to fly everywhere. "Good grief!" he shouted. "The girl's trying to scald me to death! And all because I commented on her bad history grade!"

People turned and twisted in their chairs to see what the fuss was all about.

Sabrina blushed angrily and pulled out the dishtowel she carried in her apron pocket. "I'm so sorry, Mr. Kraft," she said as she tried to dab at the coffee. "Here, let me—"

"Don't touch me!" he exclaimed, backing away from her.

Josh dashed over with some more towels and apologized as he helped Mr. Kraft dry off. Sabrina began mopping up the coffee from the table and the chairs.

"I'm supposed to be on my way to a Christmas party!" Mr. Kraft exclaimed, loud enough for everyone in the store to hear. "By the time I go home and change, I'll be late for the party." He glared at Sabrina as he pulled his sopping brown suit away from his body. "And you can be sure I'll be sending you my dry cleaning bill."

"Certainly, sir," Josh said. "Here, can I show you to another table? Can I get you another coffee?"

"Not as long as she's in the room," Kraft replied.

Ten, nine, eight, seven . . .

Sabrina tried to contain her anger as she cleaned up the spill. The whole thing was an accident. Couldn't he see? He had no right to embarrass her in front of everybody like this.

"Sabrina," Josh said, touching her on the shoulder.

"Yeah?"

"Why don't you take the rest of the night off?"

"But, Josh—"

"It's okay, Sab." He winked at her but insisted firmly, "Go ahead and clock out. Go home and watch a movie. We'll be fine here without you." Then he turned back to help Mr. Kraft.

Sabrina carried the tray to the counter. *Ten, nine, eight . . . Ten, nine, eight . . .*

Ah, forget about it, she thought miserably. She got the key and unlocked the back room where Josh had a desk and employees stashed their coats and purses while they worked.

Sabrina had dashed home after school for just a second on her way to work, and dumped her backpack while she was there. She locked up, then headed out through the coffee shop.

It felt as if a hundred pairs of eyes were on her as she made her way to the door. Josh was still fussing over Mr. Kraft.

"Maybe you should hire waitresses who can serve coffee without scalding their customers," he was saying to Josh. "You know, a lady sued that fast-food chain for a million dollars over spilled hot coffee. . . ."

Sabrina stuffed her hands in her coat pocket as she shoved through the door. Even so, the index finger on her right hand twitched.

Mr. Kraft hollered.

Sabrina tried hard not to grin.

It would be hard to prove that Mr. Kraft's slipping in a puddle of coffee on the floor had anything to do with the twitch of a teenage witch.

Out in the cold, crisp air Sabrina shuffled along the town sidewalk. Snow lay round about, crisp and deep and even, just like in the Christmas carol. It had snowed a few days before, and more was predicted. They might even have flurries tonight.

Normally Sabrina loved snow, loved the way it seemed to make everything fresh and clean and sprinkled with magic.

But tonight all she could think about was her horrible day. She'd been late for school because she'd procrastinated over getting her bad history test signed by her aunts. Aunt Zelda had insisted on lecturing her then and there. "History is one of the most important subjects for a witch," Aunt Zelda had said. "And you have no excuse with me and Hilda living in the house. We witnessed almost everything on this test. All you had to do was ask us about it."

Zelda and Hilda were several hundred years old. They'd met just about everyone from Shakespeare to Charles Dickens to Ben Franklin. But it was still history to Sabrina.

Then, just as she was about to rush off, her aunts had gotten an urgent message via Thunder and Lightning Express. They were late for a special session of the Witches' Council in the Other Realm.

"What Witches' Council meeting?" Zelda had exclaimed. "I never got a notice about it."

Salem the cat had looked up from reading his morning copy of the *Wall Street Journal*. "Maybe it was that urgent message Sabrina took out of the toaster last night when she was making frozen waffles for a bedtime snack."

Sabrina had cringed. The toaster was their mailbox from the Other Realm. "Didn't I give it to you?" she'd asked, knowing she hadn't. She'd shot her finger toward her room upstairs, and instantly the note had appeared in her hand. "Well, whaddaya know. Here it is!" She'd handed over the important message.

Zelda had slipped on her reading glasses, shaking her head as she'd read. "We were due there an hour ago! Sabrina, next time if you're going to clear our messages, please make sure you pass them on to us. If you hadn't been here when it came, we would have read it ourselves and been there on time."

"Come on, Zelda," Hilda had said as she'd zapped herself from her pj's into a dress. "Change clothes and let's go!"

Zelda had snapped her fingers and changed into a nice black suit with pearls. She'd picked up her laptop computer, then turned to Sabrina. "We'll talk more about this when we get home."

"Bye," Sabrina had said. "And sorry!"

With a flash, her aunts had disappeared.

When she'd gotten to school, the whole school was all "Santa Claus Is Coming to Town" and "Should I get something for Susie? I wasn't planning to get anything for Susie. But what if Susie gives *me* something? Then I'll be *sooo* embarrassed!"

Sabrina had felt more like "Grandma Got Run Over by a Reindeer." Especially when Mr. Kraft had given her detention for being late again.

After school, she'd hurried to her after-school job at the coffee shop. Running late, she'd mixed up her first orders.

"Can't you tell a skinny iced decaf double latte

from an extra large eggnog mochaccino?" one of her customers had asked in disdain.

It would be nice to get home.

Unless Aunt Zelda and Aunt Hilda were still mad at her. Trudging up the stairs with her backpack and purse, she spotted Salem asleep on the windowsill. *What a life,* she thought. *No history tests, no job, no timetable to keep. And all he can do is complain.*

Inside she found a note from her aunts. Unlike most human parents or guardians, Sabrina's aunts didn't pin notes to the family bulletin board or stick them to the fridge with a magnet. They left them floating in the air. She tried to ignore it, but they'd cast a trailer spell on it, and it followed her around until she snatched it out of the air to read.

> Dear Sabrina,
> We're at a Time Warp Clock Convention in the Other Realm. Not sure when it's over. Probably won't be home until at least 3 A.M.
>
> Love, Zelda and Hilda.
>
> P.S. Please leave any and all messages in the toaster for us to read when we get home.

"I need a hug," Sabrina muttered as she pinned the note back up in the air. And she knew just where to go to get it.

Harvey's house. He'd be done with basketball practice.

Maybe he could help her stop feeling like Scrooge.

She nearly ran the whole way to Harvey's house. She pounded up the porch steps and leaned on the doorbell.

Finally, she thought as she waited for him to answer the door, *something's going right about my day.*

At last Harvey opened the door. He looked tired, but she waited for his smile to light up at finding her on his doorstep. To hear him say, "Hello, Sab. I'm so glad to see you!"

But his smile seemed forced. And when he spoke, it wasn't the words she longed to hear.

"So," he said. "Where's the money?"

11

Chapter 2

☆

☆

"What money?"

Harvey frowned, something Sabrina rarely saw him do. *"The* money. As in the club money?"

At Sabrina's still blank look, he added, "The money to pay for the party and buy the presents for the kids at the Westbridge Children's Home?"

Sabrina broke out in a cold sweat. She felt sick, as if she'd eaten half a fruitcake without picking out all the weird little fake green and red cherries.

She and Harvey were in the Community Service Club at school. They donated time to charitable organizations. They worked on houses for the poor. And they had fund-raisers to earn money to donate to various causes.

This year they'd raised money to buy Christmas presents and host a huge holiday party for the kids at the Westbridge Children's Home.

Harvey was club treasurer, but he'd had basketball practice this afternoon, so Sabrina had promised Harvey she'd pick up the money from their adviser's office and drop it off at his house that evening. They wanted to go shopping in the morning to get things for the party and buy presents.

"Oh, *that* money!" Sabrina laughed nervously. "I picked it up." She bobbed her head up and down. "Just like I promised." And she had. But she'd forgotten all about bringing it over to Harvey's house.

Just don't ask me where it is—

"So where is it?" Harvey asked.

"Um . . ." Good question. Because she suddenly had no idea what she'd done with the money. "I probably put it in my purse," she said, smiling.

"Probably?"

Sabrina sneaked her hand into her small shoulder bag and felt around. *Of course it's not in there,* she told herself. *It was in a big white envelope. Bigger than your whole purse!*

She checked each of the pockets on her down jacket.

No envelope.

Quick! she told herself. *Stall. Make up an excuse. Fib!*

But a look of panic had already washed over

Harvey's face. "Don't you have it?" he squeaked out in a high voice.

"Now, now, don't panic—"

"Sabrina!"

"I know I picked it up from Mrs. Schneider's office," she explained. "I'm just not exactly sure what I did with it after that."

"What?!"

Sabrina took a step back. *Harvey just yelled,* Sabrina thought. *But Harvey never yells. This isn't good . . .*

"Sabrina!" Harvey exclaimed. "I'm responsible for that money!"

"I know, I know! Oh, Harvey, don't worry. I'm sure we'll find it. I—I probably left it at work."

"There's that word again—*probably!*" Harvey snorted. "I don't think I like that word very much."

"No, not *probably.* Did! I did leave it there. I'm sure of it! I mean, what else would I do with it?" *Good question!* she thought. But she tried to smile with confidence. "Look. I gotta go. Gotta go pick up that envelope."

Harvey grabbed his coat and tossed it on. "I'm coming with you."

"Great!" Sabrina said, keeping that smile pasted on her lips. But inside she was cringing. *Please, please, please let it be there!*

Sabrina and Harvey hurried off into the cold

night. Harvey's breath puffed out in little white clouds, but he didn't say anything as they walked along.

Seen any good movies lately? Sabrina felt like asking, but it didn't seem like a good time for idle chitchat. So she walked beside Harvey, duplicating his silence.

When they arrived at the coffee shop, Sabrina burst inside.

Several of the customers moved their coffee cups away from the tables' edges.

Sheesh, word gets around, Sabrina thought. One lousy spill and you're the Waitress from the Black Lagoon.

"Sabrina!" Josh said. "I thought I gave you the night off."

"You did," Sabrina replied. "But I think I left something here. Can I check in the back?"

"Sure." Josh handed her the key, then turned to chat with Harvey.

Sabrina hurried into the back room where she always left her coat and purse. Her hands were trembling as she fitted the key into the lock and opened the door. She rushed in and looked in the locker where she usually put her things.

Nothing there.

Maybe I laid it down somewhere when I was putting my coat on, she thought. She quickly shut the door, then turned back to the room.

Papers, books, and office junk,
Please don't think I'm funny,
Rise so I can get a peek
At where I left the money!

Sabrina waved her hand in the air. *Whoosh!*

Papers, notebooks, pencil holders, coffee cups—everything in the office slowly floated into the air. Sabrina ran around the room looking in the newly revealed places for the missing white envelope.

"Oh! I don't see it anywhere!"

After a few minutes of searching, she decided it simply wasn't there. Reluctantly she snapped her fingers.

Papers, books, and office junk,
Please don't think that I'm a bore,
Fun time's over, settle down
Exactly where you were before.

Now what? Could someone have come in and stolen the money? she wondered.

But Josh kept this back office locked when no one was in it so that employees would have a safe place to leave their coats and valuables. And Josh—no way would he have taken the money. He was definitely too cool for that.

Sabrina hated to face Harvey, but there was nothing else she could do here. With a sigh, she left the office, locked it up, then returned the key to Josh.

"Well?" Harvey asked hopefully.

"Um, maybe I left it at school."

Harvey looked as if she'd punched him in the stomach. But all he said was, "Let's go."

Sabrina was so upset that on her way out she knocked over a display of imported teas. She dropped to her knees and began to pick them up, but Josh rushed over. "That's okay, I'll take care of it. Have a good night!"

Great, Sabrina thought. *Even my own boss doesn't want me around.*

When they reached Westbridge High School, Sabrina was surprised to find the school still lit up and open.

"The Fighting Scallions shuffleboard team has a meet tonight," Harvey pointed out.

"We have a shuffleboard team?" Sabrina asked.

Harvey just gave her a look and pushed inside.

"Maybe the money's in my locker," Sabrina said brightly. She twirled the combination lock—right, left, right—and her locker swung open. The picture of Harvey she'd stuck to the inside door smiled out at her. She kept it right next to the picture of her and her mom and dad at Disney World—before the divorce. She dug through all her junk: books, papers, three pens, a little makeup bag she kept in the corner for quick touch-ups.

No white envelope.

With a sigh Sabrina locked up her locker. "Maybe Mrs. Schneider is still here. Maybe I laid it down in her office for some reason."

Together they raced to the adviser's office, but it was locked. Sabrina and Harvey peeked through the glass window, but they didn't see a white envelope on the teacher's neat, organized desk.

"Now what?" Harvey said dejectedly. "We're never going to find that money."

"Sure we are," Sabrina said. "Come on. Aunt Zelda always says if you can't find something, go back to where you were and trace your steps. Usually you find what you're looking for."

Harvey agreed, but he didn't look hopeful.

So they started at the adviser's office, then walked down the hall toward Sabrina's locker.

They went in the girls' room—well, actually, only Sabrina did. She checked the counters, checked in all the stalls, even looked through both the trash cans. But the envelope wasn't there.

"Of course I wouldn't leave it in there," Sabrina said with confidence. "Somebody might steal it."

Harvey glowered at her. "Maybe they already did."

They walked back by Sabrina's locker. They

walked slowly toward the coffee shop—they checked on the ground, in trash cans, behind bushes. From the coffee shop they headed to Harvey's house, just as Sabrina had when she'd left work. They carefully checked along the way. But when they arrived back at Harvey's house, they were still empty-handed.

Slowly they walked up onto the porch. Neither of them spoke. Sabrina felt awful.

I wish he would yell at me, she thought miserably. *But this silence. This look of total disappointment on his face . . . I can't stand it!*

"Look, Harvey," she said softly, reaching for his hand. "It'll turn up. I'm sure of it."

Harvey stuck his hand in his pocket to avoid hers. "And if it doesn't?" he said darkly.

"Well, then . . ." What could she do? "I'll—I'll cover it out of my own pocket." *There. That should make everything right.*

Harvey shot her a dubious look.

"Uh, exactly how much money did we collect?" she asked timidly.

"Six hundred and forty-seven dollars," Harvey said. "And eighty-three cents."

Sabrina cringed. *Oh, man! No way can I cover that with my bank account. I've already spent what little I had on Christmas presents. I'm almost totally broke!*

Maybe Aunt Hilda or Aunt Zelda will loan me

some money, she thought desperately. *Maybe I can work extra hours at the coffee shop.... Maybe I can blackmail Salem! I'm sure he owes me a few bucks ...*

But the worst part of the whole thing?

The look in Harvey's eyes. Sabrina would rather ski the snow-capped mountains of Mars in a bikini than face the chill factor that had suddenly invaded their usually warm and fuzzy relationship.

"I wish I'd never asked you to pick it up," Harvey muttered as he closed the door, leaving Sabrina standing on the front porch, alone, in the ice-cold night.

Sabrina flinched from the accusation. He was right. *How could I let him down like this?* she wondered. *He's right—if not for me, at least the club money would be locked up safe and sound in the adviser's office. But now ... who knows where it is?*

How will I ever get him to trust me again? Sabrina thought as she trudged through the snow toward home.

And what if I can't find the money?

Chapter 3

Sabrina poked around in the kitchen, hoping for a snack with a brand name. Witches couldn't do brand names, they could only do knockoffs. Sometimes a Hoo-Hoo was fine, but when you really felt miserable, only top-quality brand-name junk food would do.

Today had been one of the worst days of her life. And for the grand finale, she'd totally ruined things with Harvey.

But there was nothing in the cabinets—only some leftover fruitcake in a red tin decorated with an old-fashioned sleighing scene.

"Hey," she muttered. "Isn't this the same fruitcake we got from Mr. Kraft *last* Christmas?" She poked at it. Eww. It was as hard as a brick! *And where do they get these green cherries?* she wondered. She pulled one off and looked at it.

"Don't eat that!" somebody screamed.

Actually, it was the somebody in the painting on the kitchen wall. A stern-looking woman with her hair pulled back into a prim bun, dressed in old-fashioned clothes, looked out as if she were mad at the world. It had taken Sabrina months to get used to a portrait that could eavesdrop and talk back, but even now her two-dimensional relative could give her quite a scare. Sabrina figured she was often angry looking because all she got to do was hang around all day.

"Aunt Louisa! You scared me half to death," Sabrina gasped.

"Better half than all the way—from eating fruitcake," Aunt Louisa snorted. "Don't you realize no one's actually eaten a fruitcake since 1767? People just keep wrapping them up and giving them away the next year. That one there probably originated with Benjamin Franklin!"

"What are these green cherries, anyway, Aunt Louisa?"

"Is that a green cherry?" Aunt Louisa asked ominously. "Or a moldy red one?"

"Ewww!" With a shudder, Sabrina flicked the

green object into the trash. "Thanks for the warning, Aunt Louisa," Sabrina said.

"No problem," the old woman replied. "Now, if someone would just give us a homemade *buche de Noel*—now, those cakes are totally awesome!"

Sabrina went upstairs wondering if Aunt Louisa could actually eat cake. Weird. That was something she'd have to ask her aunts about.

Once in her room, Sabrina shed her coat and tossed her pocket book in the corner, then sat down at her desk and went online. *Maybe I can send Harvey an instant message,* she thought, *and apologize . . . again.* When she heard the familiar "You've got mail!" she clicked on it in delight. *Maybe Harvey's not mad at me anymore,* she thought hopefully. *Maybe he's come up with an idea. Maybe he's e-mailed me to apologize. Maybe someone's turned in the money! Maybe . . .*

She double clicked on her mailbox and scanned down her list of incoming mail. Nothing from Harvey. Not even any junk mail. Only one e-mail from an online store. She clicked it open and read:

"We're sorry, but due to an unexpected surge in pre-holiday orders, we're swamped.:)! Unfortunately your order—product number 205756762955676-L—is currently on back order. We hope to ship these items on January 13. But we value you as a customer! Please accept our apologies and this $2 gift certificate toward your next purchase . . ."

"Oh, no!" Sabrina exclaimed. "My main present for Aunt Hilda and Aunt Zelda!" Now she had nothing to give them for Christmas and few funds for doing any last-minute shopping. Especially with the club money missing.

"There's got to be some money around here!" she said as she jumped up from her chair. Frantically she began to search her room. Sabrina had a way of stuffing change and stray dollars into jean pockets and dropping it into pencil holders on her desk. Maybe she'd even tucked away some money she'd forgotten, like forgotten pirate treasure.

Too bad witches can't just zap up money! she thought. But that was totally against the rules.

Sabrina looked everywhere: the pockets of clothes in her laundry. Old coat pockets. The pink piggy bank her mother gave her in fourth grade—already raided. In the junk drawer of her dresser. Her backpack from last year—eww! No money, but a moldy sandwich in a squashed paper bag!

All total, including $2.46 in Italian lira left

over from her trip to Rome, Sabrina counted
$13.72.

Hopeless!

Just then Salem trotted in, smacking his lips.

"Where have you been?" Sabrina grumbled.

"Nowhere! Doing nothing!" Salem exclaimed
guiltily. "Can we change the subject?"

"Whatever." Salem was always up to something, but tonight she was really too upset to
care. She dropped to her knees, tossed back the
quilt, and stuck her head under her bed. Maybe
some coins—or 100 dollar bills!—had acciden-
tally fallen underneath.

Salem leaped onto the bed and peered at his
teenage witch with undisguised curiosity. Then
he purred and asked, "So where is it?"

"I don't know," Sabrina answered, her voice
muffled beneath the bed. "That's why I'm looking."

"Under the bed?" he asked. He sniffed loudly.
"I don't smell anything. Are they using new
carry-out containers?"

Sabrina backed out from under the bed and sat
back on her knees. "Salem, what are you talking
about?"

"Quit teasing me!" Salem groaned. "I'm famished!"

"So—you're always famished."

"My fish and chips!" Salem growled. "Where
is it?"

Sabrina stood up quickly and gulped. Oh, no! She'd forgotten to pick up Salem's Friday night takeout order from his favorite restaurant—Cap'n Hooks Fish and Chips—which was a couple of doors down from the coffee shop. Just one more thing she'd mucked up today!

"Um, Salem, I . . ."

"You didn't!" Salem arched his back and stared at her like an alley cat ready to pounce. "You did! You forgot!" With a shriek of dismay, the dramatic black cat collapsed on the bed and began to cry. "Boo-hoo-hoo! I've been dreaming about that meal since Tuesday! How could you forget, you mean, spoiled, selfish girl! You still have all your powers, so you can do anything. You never think of poor pitiful old me, stripped of all my magic powers for a hundred years . . ."

Sabrina winced. Salem had once been a warlock, who'd gotten caught trying to take over the world. So the Witches' Council had turned him into a cat for a hundred years and taken away all his powers but one. Too bad they'd left him with his power to speak, because he usually used it to whine and complain.

"Salem, I'm sorry I forgot—"

"But you promised!"

"I know, I know. And I'm sorry. I really am. I just have a lot of problems on my mind right now." Sabrina stroked Salem's smooth, dark hair. "Don't worry, Salem. I'll just zap you up my own recipe," she suggested. She jumped to her feet and raised her finger in the air.

"You're not a very good cook," Salem muttered.

"I've gotten better, I promise." Sabrina raised her finger again and opened her mouth to recite the incantation for deep fried seafood—

"It's not the same," Salem whined. "Zapping eliminates some of the delicate flavor. And the fries always come out a bit soggy. And it just doesn't taste as fresh as when my favorite chef deep-fries it up special, just for me. Especially since I like it with—"

"Fine!" Sabrina shouted, fed up with her miserable day. Fed up with all her horrible mistakes. Fed up with spoiled cats who only think of their tummies!

She waved her arms in the air. "Fish and chips all the way to go!" she shouted. Lightning flashed. The sound of ocean waves crashing in a storm shook the room.

And there, against her window, sat a six-foot-deep, twelve-foot-wide aquarium full of living, swimming fish of all varieties—flounder, perch, catfish, and sole—and a teeny tiny fishing pole propped up along the edge. "Fresh enough for you?!" Sabrina snapped.

Delighted, Salem leaped toward the fish tank

and perched on the windowsill. The little fishing pole was propped up like a lever, so Salem could work it with his tiny paws.

Sabrina flopped down on her bed, zapped a TV set onto her desktop—plus a satellite dish on top of the old Victorian house—and tried to lose herself in some mindless TV.

Click, click, click.

"Great," Sabrina muttered. "More than 300 channels and *It's a Wonderful Life* is playing on 267 of them."

"I love that movie!" Salem exclaimed from his perch over the perch. And flounder. "Did you see me?"

"See you?"

"Yeah, I'm in it."

"Get out of here."

"I was," Salem insisted. "I would have gotten a credit, too, but they had to cut my big scene with Donna Reed. I do show up in the crowd scene at Martini's bar and restaurant on Christmas Eve. I'm the one eating linguine with white clam sauce."

"Figures," Sabrina muttered. But tonight she was feeling too miserable to watch a movie about how wonderful life can be.

She flipped around some more.

Click, click.

The Home Shopping Channel's *Holiday Gifts Galore!*

Nope!

Click.

A wrestling organization's Holiday Special. "Peace on Earth! Goodwill toward MACHO MEN!!!" a red-faced muscle-bound Santa on steroids screamed from the screen.

"Peace on earth?" Sabrina moped. "It's a wonderful life? It's a Miserable Joke is more like it." She clicked off the TV. "Bah! Humbug!"

The phone rang. "Wonder who that could be," Sabrina muttered. "Maybe the Grinch calling to wish me a rotten Christmas. Calling to tell me he has to take my tree away so he can fix a broken light." She didn't want to talk to anybody, so she decided to ignore it. But the phone kept ringing.

Salem's black ears flicked. "Please answer it, Sabrina! You're scaring all the fish!"

With a sigh Sabrina pointed at her cordless phone and floated it to her bed. "Hello?" she asked warily.

"Sabrina, it's me."

"Harvey! Hi!" Sabrina sat up hopefully. Hopefully Harvey had had a change of heart. They'd make up, then solve the problem of the missing money . . . together.

But the only thing Harvey said was, "Did you find the money yet?"

Sabrina's heart sank. "Not exactly," she hedged.

"You mean no."

"Well . . . yeah."

Silence on the other end of the phone. Then a big, deep sigh. "I'm going to have to quit school," he muttered, "get a job, earn the money to pay them back . . ."

"Harvey—"

Click. Too late. He'd already hung up the phone. *I'll call him back,* she thought as she clicked off the phone to get a dial tone. *Explain . . . make excuses . . . promise him . . .*

What? Sabrina dropped the phone on the bed. She could think of nothing to say that would make it better—nothing that would make the coldness disappear from Harvey's voice. Nothing that would un-disappoint him and make him trust her again.

And with a true, honest guy like Harvey, trust wasn't something you could win back with a snap of your fingers. It would take more than magic tricks to make him ever trust her again.

"He probably wishes he never met me," Sabrina muttered unhappily. She fell back on her bed, groaning in despair. "I wish I'd never been born!" she moaned as hot tears leaked from the corners of her eyes.

There was a very good reason Sabrina's aunts kept a magnet on the refrigerator that said

Be Careful What You Wish For: You Might Get It.

But Sabrina wasn't in the kitchen. And she wasn't thinking about the Other Realm. Her mind was only on the human world and the very human problems of a teenage girl.

"Sabrina, my love, *n-o-o-o-o-o!*" Outside her window, Roland the lovesick troll trembled as he clung to the ivy that climbed the wall of the old Victorian home. Sweat poured down his wrinkled brow as he struggled *not* to grant Sabrina's wish. "Must—resist—," he gasped. "Can't grant . . . that wish—"

Normally Roland the troll was very stingy about granting wishes, but he'd gotten in trouble with the Witches' Council again and they'd levied a punishment. They knew the one thing he hated most was to give away wishes. So his punishment was this: He must grant the very next wish he heard—whatever it was.

He'd hurried over to Sabrina's house. He really had a major crush on her. And he figured that as long as he *had* to grant a wish, he'd make sure he was in a position to grant one for Sabrina. Sort of a present to her. Surely *that* would make her fall into his arms!

Only now look! She'd gone and wished for something really awful. She'd wished she'd never been born!

Roland fought with all his might. He struggled and strained. He tried to use every trick of mind control he'd ever learned.

But it was no use. What's the will of one tiny troll against the magic of the entire Witches' Council?

Roland was powerless to resist.

Sabrina was going to get her wish.

Chapter 4

"Sabrina!"

"Roland?"

"My fish!" Salem cried.

Roland burst in through the window, granted Sabrina's wish—*BOING!*—then, in his distress, tumbled into the six-foot-deep aquarium. Which was pretty deep for a guy who was only a yard-stick tall.

"Help! Hel—glub!" He sank in the water, then bobbed to the surface, splashing frantically. "Help!" he gasped. "I can't swim!"

Sabrina stared at him. "You live under a bridge and you can't swim?"

"I never learned," he sputtered. "I was too

33

scared of snakes . . . glub, glub . . . and those lit-tle icky tadpole things!"

Ignoring her shock at Roland's sudden appear-ance, Sabrina got to her feet, bounced three times on her bed (Zelda always told her not to jump on her bed, but this was an emergency!), and on the third bounce dived like an Olympic swimmer into the tank.

The water was cold and slimy and full of fish—not exactly a nice dip in the pool!—but Sabrina managed to grab hold of the squirming troll and drag him out of the water.

Salem shivered as he shook off the water droplets that had splattered his sleek black coat. He hated water almost as much as he hated the fact that he'd been changed into a powerless cat for a hundred years. "I don't get it, Sabrina," he said. "If I still had my powers, I'd simply have whisked him out of the water with a snap of my fingers—without subjecting myself to the dis-comfort of a dunk in the water."

"Oh, yeah." Sabrina looked down at her drenched clothing and at the sopping wet troll drip-ping water all over her bedroom floor. Sometimes she forgot. After all, she'd only been aware of her witch half for a couple of years, but she'd been human for nearly two decades; in emergencies, she sometimes reacted as a human first, witch second.

Roland's teeth chattered as he hugged his arms

to his chest. "H-how about using your m-m-magic to take c-c-care of the quick dry, hmm?"

A troll is dripping all over my bed.
I'm dripping all over my floor.
Send me a wind to dry us both off,
Then don't let us drip anymore.

Suddenly a warm Western wind blew through the room. It felt a little like going through the drying section of a drive-through car wash, but it worked even faster.

"Oh, thank you, Sabrina darling!" Roland exclaimed, kissing her hand. "And . . . I'm sorry."

Sabrina jerked her hand out of his grasp. "If you're talking about slobbering on my hand, you're not excused. Don't do it again." Then, worried she might have hurt his feelings, she added more kindly, "And if you're talking about falling into the aquarium and getting my room wet, well, don't worry about it. It wasn't your fault, and everything's dry again."

"Easy for you to say," Salem muttered from his seat near the aquarium. "He's scared all the fish!"

Roland's eyes shifted and he wrung his sleeve, even though there was no longer any water to wring from it. "Uh, actually, I was apologizing for something else." He lowered his eyes and dropped his voice. "The wish," he mumbled.

Sabrina leaned forward, trying to hear. "The fish?"

Roland shook his head. "The *wish.*"

"What wish?"

Roland turned away from her and swallowed hard. "I had to do it," he insisted. "It was part of my punishment."

Sabrina folded her arms and glared at the little man. "Do what, Roland?"

"Uh . . ."

"Come on, Roland! Spit it out. What have you done this time?"

Roland screwed up his courage and blurted, "I had to grant your wish."

"Wish?" Sabrina looked even more puzzled. "What wish? I don't remember making any wish." Suddenly her eyes lit up. "You mean when I wished I could go to the N'Sync concert even though Zelda and Hilda said because of the grade I got on my last history exam I couldn't go?"

"Uh . . . not that wish."

Sabrina thought hard. "Harvey! Did I wish he wasn't mad at me?" she asked hopefully.

"You mean Farm Boy?" Roland glared. He'd met Harvey Kinkle on a few occasions and taken an instant dislike to him, mostly because Harvey seemed to hold Sabrina's affection when he himself could do nothing to win her love. Then he suddenly smiled. "He's mad at you? That's great news!"

"Roland!"

"Okay, okay," he said, holding up his hands. "No, I didn't grant that wish, because if you wished it, you never wished it out loud. And under the rules and regulations governing the spell I was put under by the Witches' Council, I had to grant the first wish I heard spoken aloud."

"I don't remember making any wish!" Sabrina exclaimed, her voice rising in frustration. "Just tell me!"

Roland drew himself up to his full height and straightened his gold-braided jacket. "You've never been born," he announced.

"What?!"

Roland shrugged. "You don't exist."

Sabrina stared at the little troll a moment, then burst out laughing. "Oh, good one, Roland. You had me really going there for a minute. This is some kind of joke, isn't it? Who put you up to this? Salem? Cousin Amanda?"

"No, no, they have nothing to do with it," Roland insisted. With a deep sigh he took Sabrina's hand and stared up into her eyes. "Don't you remember, my darling? Just before I tumbled into the aquarium, you shouted out, 'I wish I'd never been born!' "

"Oh, *that*," Sabrina chuckled. "I didn't really *mean* it."

Roland shrugged. "You said it, sweetie. I didn't have a choice. You shouldn't play around with wishes when there's a troll around. It's dangerous!"

"Wait a minute, Roland. You're not making any sense." Sabrina looked down at herself, standing there. Her toes were still encased in her newest black leather boots. Her jean-clad legs still stood there. She held her hands up in front of her face and wiggled her fingers. She ran her fingers over her face and felt her eyes, nose, and mouth still in the right places. She snapped her fingers, clapped her hands, stamped her feet. "I feel pretty real to me."

Roland stroked his stubby brown beard. "Yeah, I don't exactly get that part, either." Then he suddenly grabbed Sabrina by the hands and twirled around with her. "But hey, I can still see you, so who cares about the technicalities." He dropped to his knees and smiled up into her eyes. "Now will you marry me? You might as well. You don't exist to anybody else."

"Stop that!" Sabrina scolded Roland. "We've been through all that before. And I still don't believe you." Then her eyes narrowed as she glared at the happy little troll. "I get it. This is just some sick joke of yours to get me to marry you—"

"No, Sabrina my love, I promise!"

"Salem," she said, turning toward the aquarium, "tell this little troll that he's out of his . . ."

Sabrina's voice trailed off when she realized Salem wasn't there. In fact, the entire aquarium had totally disappeared.

"Hey, who did that?" Sabrina exclaimed. "Who got rid of the aquarium?"

"Sabrina," Roland said firmly as he waved his arm around her room, "just look!"

Sabrina stopped complaining long enough to look around her bedroom. "Hey, where's my lava light?" she exclaimed. "And my teddy bear?" She whirled around. "Hey—where's all my stuff?"

Something really strange was going on. All of Sabrina's things had totally disappeared: her CD player, the bedspread she'd picked out herself, all the clothes she'd left lying around.

"It doesn't even look like my room anymore," she said. "It looks like a guest room."

Roland tried to slip a sympathetic arm around Sabrina's waist, but he couldn't reach it. So he settled for patting her on the knee. "That's because it *is* a guest room, Sabrina my fairest one. This is not your room because you don't exist. You were never born, so you never came here to live with your aunts. This is a guest room . . ." He ran his hand over the dresser top, and his fingers came away covered with dust. "And by the looks of it, no one's slept here for a long, long time."

He snorted. "It's no wonder, the way Hilda and Zelda treat their guests from the Other Realm."

Sabrina ran to her closet and jerked open the door.

Empty! . . . except for a couple of half-used rolls of gift wrap and an old abacus stuck in a corner.

"No . . . ," she said, shaking her head.

She dashed to her dresser and frantically began yanking open the drawers. Top, middle, third one down, bottom . . .

Sabrina sank to her knees on the old, dusty rug.

Empty. All empty.

With trembling fingers she slowly shoved the bottom drawer closed. For a moment she just sat there, her hands still grasping the knobs, as she tried to make sense of what she was seeing.

Then she jumped to her feet and whirled around. "It won't work, Roland."

"What, Sabrina my love? The drawer? Let me help you—"

"No! Your sick joke. You did all this. You made all my stuff disappear—my clothes, my knickknacks, my CDs, my makeup."

"Why would I do that?" Roland gasped.

"You're trying to trick me into your arms," Sabrina accused him. "Trying to trick me into marrying you. You got rid of my stuff and got me all confused so I'd turn to you for help and marry you out of gratitude."

"No, Sabrina—"

"Well, let me tell you, you mean old troll! It won't work! Because I wouldn't marry you if you were the last troll—I mean, guy!—on earth!"

Sabrina turned toward the door. "Just wait till I tell Aunt Hilda and Aunt Zelda about this. Just wait till I—"

Roland toddled around and threw himself between Sabrina and the door. "Sabrina. Wait. Believe me—"

"Forget it, pal. I'm—"

"Sabrina. Just look."

Something in Roland's voice made Sabrina stop. She let him lead her over to the full-length mirror that she had on her closet door.

And when she looked into the mirror—the mirror she used to check out her hair and clothes every morning before school—she couldn't believe her eyes.

There was nothing there.

Chapter 5

Sabrina felt as if she'd fallen off her flying vacuum cleaner and had the wind knocked out of her lungs.

Where am I? . . .

She touched the cool surface of the mirror where the image of her face should be. Where her hand should be reflected.

Nothing. It was as if she were invisible.

Roland was polite enough not to say anything at that moment. He just looked up at her with his dark brown eyes.

"But—," Sabrina sputtered, "how come *I* can see me? How come *you* can see me if I'm really not here?"

Roland rubbed his forehead as if he felt a

headache coming on. "Please, I flunked all my science courses at Troll School—don't ask me to explain. All I know is that I had to grant your wish—and you wished you'd never been born. But why fight it?" He slid up beside her and laced his stubby fingers through hers. "All I know is that I'm glad I can still see you. Who cares about the rest of the world? Come with me to my home beneath the bridge, and we'll live happily every after. Whether you possess a valid birth certificate or not is not important to me."

Sabrina tore her hand from his grasp. "Can you be serious for a minute!" she exclaimed.

Roland shrugged. "I am."

Sabrina began to pace back and forth in the room—the room that should have felt comforting and familiar, a room that felt like it belonged to a stranger. "Okay, one step at a time here. Weirder things have happened to me since I moved in with Aunt Zelda and Aunt Hilda and learned I was a witch. Talking pictures, time travel—maybe this is just some sort of weird *Star Trek* kind of Other Realm static interference . . . or something."

Roland patted her hand. "You're raving now, Sabrina. Let me take you home and serve you a nice mug of grog. I make it using water from my own bog."

"Ewww." Sabrina shook her head and pinched herself. When she didn't wake up—when everything stayed the same—she seemed to come to a decision. "Sorry, Roland. But I can prove I still exist. I'll just find somebody—somebody who knows me. That'll prove you're wrong."

"I wish I were," he replied sadly.

"Dad!" Sabrina said, snapping her fingers. What better way to prove you were born than having a friendly chat with a parent? And her father was easy to find. He was in the book—literally. The book *The Discovery of Magic,* which her aunts had given her on her sixteenth birthday when they'd informed her of her dual heritage. All she had to do was look him up under S, and she'd find his handsome face smiling back at her from a black-and-white photo. But that wasn't all. The picture would come to life and she could actually talk with him, sort of like a supernatural version of a videophone.

She turned and dashed toward her desk where she usually kept the book for quick reference.

It wasn't there.

Gone—just like all my other stuff!

Daddy! Sabrina felt worry snake through her heart. The book was her one sure hot line to her father whenever she needed his help. Now her connection to her father was missing.

"See?" Roland said. "You never got *The Discovery of Magic* for your sixteenth birthday because—"

"Yeah, yeah, I know, I know. I never had a birthday because I was never born!"

"Now you're catching on!" Roland said cheerfully.

"No, I'm not," Sabrina insisted. "If only I could talk to Dad . . ."

"But Ted Spellman isn't your dad," Roland said. "In fact, he doesn't have any children because—"

"*Please* don't say that again!"

"But it's—"

"*Not* true," she insisted fervently. "This is simply some kind of test—I'm sure of it. I'll—I'll—Just let me think a minute. I'll figure it all out."

"You're beautiful when you're being forceful."

"Aaaggghhh!"

Okay, calm down, Sabrina told herself. *Ignore the passes. Just try to think what to do next.*

Her aunts were off in the Other Realm at a Time Warp Clock Convention until 3:00 A.M.

I guess I could go through the linen closet and try to find them, she thought. The Spellmans' upstairs linen closet was their express train to the Other Realm.

But they could be anywhere, Sabrina thought. *And it could take forever to find them.*

And then a single word filled her heart and mind. *Harvey.*

"That's it!" Sabrina exclaimed happily. "I'll go

over to Harvey's house. He's so mad at me! And when he yells at me, it'll be *proof* I still exist."

"So, you'll take Farm Boy's word over mine, hmm?" Roland stamped his foot. But when he saw Sabrina head for the stairs, he chased after her. "Hey, wait for me! If you get lost, I'll never be able to find you—since you don't exist!"

Sabrina stuffed her hands in the pockets of her jacket and walked briskly through the icy night air. The snow glistened in pools of light shed by the streetlamps. The houses she passed glowed cheerfully with Christmas lights and other decorations, but Sabrina was in too bad a mood to enjoy their beauty. Roland ran along behind her, huffing and puffing and muttering strange oaths about frogs and goats beneath his breath. When at last they reached Harvey's, Sabrina noticed that the house seemed dark and quiet.

"I don't see any lights on," Roland pointed out. "Maybe no one's home. Maybe they're asleep. Come on," he said, tugging on her arm. "Let's go."

But Sabrina pulled away. "I don't care," she insisted. "I *have* to see Harvey! And he can't get any angrier at me than he already is."

Sabrina pounded up the steps and jabbed the doorbell. *Ding-ding-ding-ding-ding!*

At first she wondered if anyone was home. But

then she heard someone coming. Seconds later Sabrina squinted as the porch light winked on.

The door opened a narrow crack. "Yes?" said a woman's voice.

"Mrs. Kinkle! It's me—Sabrina!"

The woman peered at her, frowning. "Who?" She shook her head. "I don't buy anything door to door—"

"But I'm not selling anything—"

"And we don't give to charity that way, either. My husband gave at the office." She yawned and started to close the door, but Sabrina stuck the toe of her boot in the way just in time. *Why doesn't she recognize me?* Sabrina wondered. *Maybe it's too dark,* she tried to tell herself. *Maybe she's too sleepy . . .*

"Now, look here," Mrs. Kinkle said, frowning. "It's late, too late to be ringing doorbells. If you don't leave, I'll get my husband—"

"Can I just talk to Harvey, please, Mrs. Kinkle?"

The woman glared at her. "Harvey? What do you want with him? Does he know you?"

Fear rose in Sabrina's throat. Mrs. Kinkle seemed not to know her at all. *But I can't think about that right now. I've got to find Harvey. Harvey will know me. And—angry or not—he'd help.* "I'm a friend of his," Sabrina explained. "From school. I really need to speak to him."

"School? Hmph! He doesn't go there anymore," Mrs. Kinkle muttered.

What? Sabrina didn't understand. *What was going on?*

"Please, Mrs. Kinkle," Sabrina said, trying to be as polite as possible. "I just need to speak to Harvey. It's very important."

"Harvey's gone," Mrs. Kinkle said darkly.

"Wh-what do you mean?" Sabrina asked. *Doesn't go to school. He's gone... Oh, my gosh! Have they arrested him for the missing club money?*

"He and his dad had a fight when he dropped out of school," Mrs. Kinkle revealed, her voice suddenly thick with emotion. "Harvey doesn't live here anymore. He's moved out—for good."

Chapter 6

"**M**oved out?" Sabrina exclaimed. "When? Tonight?"

"Weeks ago," Harvey's mother said, her voice nearly a whisper. She sounded as if she were about to cry.

Sabrina couldn't believe it. Harvey had moved away from home weeks ago, and yet he'd never said a word to her? It didn't make sense. "Where does he live?" she asked Mrs. Kinkle.

"He moved to an apartment," Mrs. Kinkle replied. "I think it's called the Tattered Arms."

"What's his apartment number?"

But Mrs. Kinkle was closing the door again. "I've told you too much already. Go on now, or I'll call the cops to chase you away." She peered out into the darkness. "And take your little brother with you!"

"Okay—fine. No problem." Sabrina held up her hands, backing away slowly. She didn't want trouble, especially from Harvey's mother. "Come on, Roland," she said as she hurried down the steps. "We've got to find Harvey and find out what's going on."

Roland followed, grumbling. "Little brother? Hmph! I'm at least a hundred years older than you. . . . And Sabrina, we know what's going on. . . ."

Out beneath the streetlight, Sabrina glanced around. The streets looked empty. Satisfied that no one was watching, she pointed her gloved finger at her pocket.

What I need is a Westbridge map,
with apartments listed—when I snap!

Roland made a face at her lame poetry, but she didn't care—as long as the magic worked. She snapped her fingers and instantly felt a folded paper appear in her pocket. She quickly pulled it out and unfolded it. "Yes! A map of Westbridge." She held it up to the light and noticed a big circle made with a red felt-tipped marker around the words Tattered Arms Apartments. "Here it is," she told Roland. "At the corner of Robert Down Avenue and Out Street."

"At the corner of Down and Out?" Roland chortled. "That's funny!"

But Sabrina didn't think it was funny—not if Harvey lived there. She studied the map and frowned. "That's on the other side of town."

Roland groaned. "Can we take the subway?"

"There's no subway in Westbridge," Sabrina informed the little troll. "But I can get you a seat on the Witch Express." She hooked a finger under the troll's collar, then snapped her fingers again. "Hang on!"

Zzzzzzzap!

An instant later they stood at the corner of Down and Out. The Tattered Arms was an old, shabby apartment building with trash blowing across the snowy yard and bars on the windows. Someone had taped a piece of cardboard over a broken window upstairs. Shivering, Sabrina hurried into the entryway with Roland right behind her.

Oh, Harvey! Sabrina thought. Why was he living here when he had a wonderful home he could share with his mother and father? And why hadn't he told her about it?

Sabrina pushed through the front door into the entryway. It was dark and shadowy. All but one of the lightbulbs up on the stairs had burned out. How could she find out which apartment was

Harvey's? She could try to think up a magic spell to discover his whereabouts, but she saw something that might be quicker.

Mailboxes.

Beneath each one was a tiny brass slot where a piece of paper with a name written on it could be inserted. She could barely read the names in the dim light, so she zapped a flashlight into her hands and shone it across the labels. Some were missing. Others were yellow and faded with age, as if the residents had lived here a long, long time. So the new white card beneath one mailbox stood out like a full moon on a dark night. Written on it in neat but boyish print was the name H. Kinkle.

"It's him!" Sabrina exclaimed, happy to have found him but sad to discover that he really lived here. "Apartment 5G. Come on, Roland. I'll prove to you I still exist. Harvey will know me. Harvey will know me for sure." She took the stairs two at a time in her rush to reach him.

Roland scowled at the dingy walls. "The things a troll has to do to find true love," he muttered. Then he heaved a small sigh and followed. Each single step was like two at a time for him. It was going to be a long climb. "Why would anybody want to live on the fifth floor," muttered the troll, who lived beneath a bridge. "Is it a sublet from Rapunzel or something?"

At last Sabrina reached the fifth floor. Something scuttled across the floor. A rat? "Rats don't climb this high, do they, Roland?" Sabrina whispered.

Roland shrieked and threw himself into Sabrina's arms. "Of course they can!" he exclaimed.

"Roland!" she hissed. "This is no time to get romantic!" She twisted free of his iron grasp and set him back down on the ground. He still clung to her leg, but at least she had her hands free.

Urgently she knocked on the door of apartment 5G.

The door remained closed.

Sabrina pressed her ear to the door and listened. She could hear the faint sounds of a television. It sounded like cartoons.

"Harvey!" Sabrina pounded on the door again. "Harvey, it's me. Sabrina!"

At last she heard movement. Someone unlocked several locks, chains, dead bolts. Then the door creaked open and Harvey peeked out. "Yeah?"

"Harvey!" Sabrina gushed in relief.

"Who wants to know?" Harvey asked suspiciously.

"Harvey, it's me—Sabrina!" she exclaimed. Maybe he couldn't see her well in the dim hall light.

He peered at her, frowning.

"Oh, Harvey, don't you know me?"

"What'd you say your name was?"

"Sabrina. You know—Sab?" she said, hoping his nickname for her would make him realize who she was.

"I don't know any Sabrina," he said and started to shut the door.

"Wait!" She jammed her hand and boot into the doorway. "It's me, your girlfriend? The girl you've sat next to in the cafeteria nearly every day for the past several years? The girl who cheered for you at every football game, basketball game, and track meet you ever participated in for the Fighting Scallions?"

"I don't go to school," Harvey said glumly. "I quit. And I never played sports when I was there. I never made any of them teams."

Sabrina's mind reeled. What was he talking about? Harvey always played sports—every sport. He'd scored three baskets in the basketball game just last week. "But when did you quit school?"

Harvey shrugged. "I dunno. Six months ago, maybe. Now I work down at Sam's Garage—I'm learning to be a mechanic."

"But that's impossible!" Sabrina exclaimed. "I've seen you at school—you were there today!" Sabrina insisted. "You're treasurer for the Community Service Club. What about the lost money?"

Harvey looked nervous now and tried to close the door. "I don't know anything about any money," he said, "and I don't know you—or your little brother."

"I'm not her brother!" Roland shouted. "I'm her new boyfriend."

Sabrina ignored Roland's remark and struggled to keep the door open. "Harvey! I'm sorry you're mad at me about the club money. But please, don't act this way—it isn't funny. I'm Sabrina! Tell me you know who I am!"

"I tell you I *don't* know anybody named Sabrina!" Harvey insisted and slammed the door in her face. Sabrina could hear the five locks, chains, and dead bolts as they clicked into place.

And she heard Harvey's final words, muffled through the thick locked door: "I never met a Sabrina in my whole life. Now go away and leave me alone!"

Chapter 7

"Don't cry, Sabrina," Roland said, patting Sabrina on the shoulder as tears pooled in her eyes. "After all, you've still got me."

Sitting on the front porch steps of the Tattered Arms, Sabrina burst into sobs.

"Think of it this way," Roland went on. "Farm Boy there was never really right for you. You're half witch—he's only human. He could never really be a part of your world or truly understand you. You'd never be happy with him. Didn't your own parents' divorce teach you that?"

"Don't talk about my parents!" Sabrina snapped between sobs. She couldn't believe it. Harvey really didn't know who she was. Had something happened to make him forget her? A car accident? A bump on the head playing sports?

Or ... maybe the fact that you were never born? suggested a tiny voice inside her head.

"No!" Sabrina cried. "It can't be true!"

"Maybe it is," Roland said.

"Even if it was, Harvey should be the same. But he's so different," Sabrina said. "He's usually so happy and cheerful. But now he seems so ... so depressed. And he loves sports. Why wouldn't he play sports?"

"I guess without you around to cheer him on, Harvey never made any of the teams," Roland said. "Maybe knowing you was what made him so cheerful. Looks like you made a difference in the guy's life. Except ... not now, now that you've wished it all away. He never knew you, because you don't exist, and his life's turning out a different way."

Sabrina snapped her fingers, and a hankie appeared in her hand so she could dab her eyes. "Quit saying I don't exist!" she said. "It's very rude. And besides, I'm here, aren't I? Things are just all mixed up." She sniffed. "I just wish I could talk to my dad. He'd know what to do. . . ."

If you don't like where you are and what's going on, take one giant step forward—and you'll immediately have a new point of view.

Sabrina smiled. That was something her dad had always told her when she was growing up.

Don't whine!

Now she laughed out loud. That was another thing he'd been fond of saying!

So her dad wasn't here and she didn't know how to get in touch with him, but she *could* remember the things he'd always told her. That was almost as good as being able to talk to him.

And it was good advice. *Sitting here feeling sorry for myself won't get me anywhere,* she said to herself. She blew her nose with her hankie, snapped her fingers to make it disappear, then got to her feet. "Come on!" she told Roland.

"Now where are we going?" Roland said. "It's late, and it's cold. Come on, Sabrina. Forget about Harry—"

"That's Harvey!"

"Who cares? He doesn't know you anymore. Come back with me to my snug little house beneath the bridge. I'll make you a nice, warm fire."

"Not a chance," Sabrina said. "I've got too much to do. I've got to prove that I really exist!"

Within seconds Sabrina had whisked them to the front of Westbridge High School. She checked carefully to see if anyone was around. But since it was nighttime, and there were no school events this evening, the tall, redbrick building was dark and quiet, with only a few security lights on.

"What are we doing here?" Roland said. "Schools give me the creeps—even when they're closed!"

"School records," Sabrina replied. "That'll prove my existence. They keep records of everything. You'll see."

Sabrina zapped them into the school building, where she stopped in front of a bank of lockers. "See? This is my locker," she whispered to Roland. She quickly snapped a flashlight into Roland's hand. "Hold that for me, so I can see."

Sabrina's combination lock glinted in the light of the flashlight as she spun the correct numbers to unlock it.

But when she pulled on it, it wouldn't open. "Heh, I guess I'm a little nervous," she said, "with all that's been happening." Quickly she turned the dial again. To the right, to the left, to the right again. Pull—

It *still* wouldn't open! "What's wrong with this thing?" She yanked on it, hard. Still no luck. In frustration, she gave it a quick zap with her finger, which immediately opened it. She shrugged apologetically to Roland. "I don't have all night."

But when she looked inside the locker—*her* locker—her mouth fell open in surprise. "Hey! Where's all my stuff?" Her books were all gone.

So was the picture of Harvey and the one of her with her mom and dad when they took her to Disney World, before their divorce, the little makeup bag she kept in the corner for quick touch-ups, and the little magnet that said FRIENDS 4-EVER that her old friend Valerie had given her when she'd moved away . . .

None of it was there. Nothing to prove it had ever been her locker.

Instead there was a poster of some polka band—*definitely* not hers!—dozens of candy wrappers, and a paper bag full of—*Phew!*—boy's gym clothes that didn't appear to have been washed since the beginning of the school year.

"Somebody stole my locker!" Sabrina cried.

"Maybe it's not your locker," Roland said gently. "Your combination didn't work on the lock. And it's not your stuff."

"So? Somebody must have moved my things. Changed the lock. So what?" Sabrina said angrily. "It's still *my* locker. I should know. It's the same one I've used every day of school since my first day at Westbridge. See? It's got this little dent down on the bottom right corner from when I—"

Sabrina broke off as she stared at the corner.

It was completely dent free.

"I don't care!" Sabrina wailed. "It's my locker and I want it back!" She zapped all the stuff in the locker into a brown paper bag and left it lying on the floor—along with the obnoxious combination lock. "That'll teach whoever to mess around in my locker."

Then she waved her finger and the locker filled with sparkles. A picture of Harvey appeared on the inside locker door. And the picture of her mom and dad at Disney World.

Wait a minute! A picture of her mom and dad at Disney World—by *themselves?* "I'm not in the picture anymore!" she cried. She held it up for Roland to see, but he just shrugged.

"What's it going to take to make you believe me?" he asked.

Sabrina tossed the picture into the locker and slammed it shut. Then she ran toward the office.

I've got to see my file!

She ran down the hallway.

Roland rolled his eyes. "Not again!" He took a deep breath and followed after her. "She's definitely going to have to cut down on the running after we're married."

When they neared the office, Sabrina slowed down. She heard voices.

It sounded like Principal Kraft and . . .

Libby Chessler?

Impossible! Sabrina thought. The ex-head cheerleader and all-around obnoxious snob got shipped off to boarding school. *She doesn't even go here anymore.*

Sabrina peeked around the corner into the office.

It was Libby all right. She and Mr. Kraft were having a deep discussion about something. What was she doing here? And the files Sabrina wanted to look in were behind the secretary's desk in the outer office. If she went in now, they'd see her.

Unless . . . I make myself invisible . . .

Time for some witch work. "Stay here," she ordered Roland. Then she folded her arms and said a spell:

There are things I need to see and hear,
So make Sabrina disappear.

Sabrina felt a shiver down in the electrons of her being, then with a shudder, like a dog shaking water from his coat, she was invisible.

"Can you see me at all, Roland?" Sabrina whispered.

"No, but I carry your beautiful image in my heart forever," Roland tried.

"Sheesh, you never let it rest, do you?"

"Not till you're mine, my sweet."

Sabrina ignored him and tiptoed into the outer secretary's office. She had to be careful because even though the spell made her invisible, it didn't disguise the sound of her boots on the linoleum floor.

Once inside, Sabrina paused. The doorway that led from this office into Mr. Kraft's office was situated so that he couldn't see the file cabinets in the corner behind the secretary's desk—as long as he stayed seated at his own desk.

She paused and studied a curious picture on the wall. WESTBRIDGE HIGH SCHOOL UNIFORMS read the caption. Beneath that was a photograph of two students—a boy and a girl—showing the proper way to wear the school uniforms and accessories.

"Eww," Sabrina couldn't help but whisper. *Who picked those out? They go way beyond fashion mistakes—they're fashion crimes!* For the girls, pleated plaid wool skirts worn with a plain white short-sleeved shirt *tucked in* and a wide, shapeless navy blue vest. Plus navy blue knee socks. It was a look that would make even the thinnest, most beautiful high school girl look like a fat fourth grader.

The boy's navy blue suit and solid navy tie looked like something out of the 1950s.

Was this something new Mr. Kraft had planned to torture the student body with?

It'll never work, Sabrina thought. *Nobody at this school will put up with that. Except maybe Ronald Persley, who kind of dresses like that anyway.*

But Sabrina couldn't worry about all that now. She had to get into those files!

But when she passed the secretary's desk, she gasped softly. A large picture in a silver frame sat on the corner of the desk—a picture of the secretary and Mr. Kraft in the clothes of a bride and groom, with their arms wrapped around each other.

Mr. Kraft married his secretary? Married? But . . . when? What about him and Aunt Zelda?

Sabrina admired her Aunt Zelda immensely and thought she had one of the finest scientific minds on Earth or in the Other Realm. But for some strange, inexplicable reason she was dating Mr. Kraft. Sabrina could never understand how such a brilliant woman could fall in with a man like that.

And now it looked as if the dirty rat had run off with his secretary!

Well, that's just great! Sabrina thought, shaking her head. Then, *Actually, that is just great!* Of course, Sabrina didn't want Aunt Zelda's feelings to be hurt, but she knew Aunt Zelda deserved something better, and Sabrina was secretly glad she'd never have Mr. Kraft for an uncle!

Slowly, carefully she tiptoed to the filing cabinet behind the secretary's desk. She searched till she found the drawer with the letters S–U. Then slowly she wrapped her fingers around the drawer handle and began to pull. Slowly . . . millimeter by millimeter . . . so as not to make any sound.

As she worked at easing open the drawer, she listened in on Mr. Kraft and Libby's conversation.

"I think the uniforms I picked are working out just fine," Libby told the vice principal. "After six months in use, I've noticed it's really helped with school noise. Everyone's so embarrassed by their uniforms, they sit quietly at their desks, trying not to attract any attention, so no one looks at how bad they look!" Libby laughed as only a head cheerleader could.

Mr. Kraft murmured in agreement. "Although . . . occasionally some students ask me why you don't have to wear one."

"Me?" Libby exclaimed. "I'd look terrible in those tacky clothes! Besides, since I've abolished the positions of homecoming queen and student body president and become school dictator, it's important that I stand out from the crowd, so students can easily identify me. In case they have any questions."

Kraft held up his hands. "Okay. Fine. Just asking."

Libby glared at him, then went down her list. "Now, next issue . . ."

"Uh, excuse me." Mr. Kraft raised his hand like a little boy who needed to go to the bathroom.

Libby flipped her glossy dark hair over her shoulder and glared. "Yes?"

"Um, it's getting rather late, and I did have this Christmas party I was supposed to take my wife to tonight—"

"Hey, if you're too busy to do the job right, my daddy and I can always find a new principal to take your place."

"No, no!" Mr. Kraft replied quickly. He shoved his thick glasses up on his nose. "I hate Christmas parties anyway. All that eggnog. All those cookies with the green and red icing . . ." He shivered in pretend disgust. "Your next item was? . . ."

Sabrina couldn't believe it. She knew that when Libby used to go to school at Westbridge High, she could always twist Mr. Kraft around her little finger and get him to do whatever she wanted him to do. But all this—uniforms, class dictator, treating him as if he worked for her—this was really bizarre.

And what was she talking about . . . the uniforms were "working out"? *We don't wear uniforms at Westbridge.* All this was making Sabrina's head hurt. *Better just get my file and get out of here,* she told herself.

But the next words out of Libby's mouth sent a winter chill through Sabrina's heart and froze her to the spot.

"Harvey," Libby said.

"What about him?" Mr. Kraft asked nervously.

"You've simply *got* to reinstate him," Libby said firmly. "He's got to graduate."

"But I can't!" Mr. Kraft cried. "He quit school of his own free will. Just think of the paperwork to get him back in! And besides, before that his grades were the lowest ever recorded in the history of this school. He doesn't belong here in my school. He'll be much happier finding a trade that he can—"

"*Your* school?" Libby interrupted, her left eyebrow arched.

"*Your* school," Mr. Kraft whispered obediently.

Libby nodded. "Exactly. My daddy gave it to me for my fourteenth birthday. So don't you forget it. And as for where Harvey would be happiest, that's not the issue here. *I'm* not 'happier' with him gone. I've already made plans for Harvey and me to become officially engaged at graduation—on the stage, after we both receive our diplomas. Daddy's already . . . shall we say 'obtained' two spots in a choice East Coast university, and I've already scheduled a church and hotel for the wedding and reception to be held the day after college graduation. It just doesn't work for me for Harvey to be a high school dropout or"—she shivered in distaste—"a mechanic."

"Hey, I'd love to have a good mechanic in the family," Mr. Kraft said.

"Well, *I* have to marry a college *graduate*," Libby insisted.

"But, Libby, please, be reasonable," Mr. Kraft whined. "The boy just isn't a student. And he seems to me to be a very depressed young man."

"Nonsense," Libby said. "He's only been a little depressed since, well . . . since about the time I started dating him, actually. I'm not sure why. But not to worry—a friend of my mom's, Dr. Nordmeyer? He'll fix Harvey right up."

"But, Libby, still, his grades—"

"And *you'll* fix *those* right up. Right?" Libby asked it as a question. But something in her voice made it an order, not a request.

Mr. Kraft's office chair squeaked as he sank back into it in resignation. "Of course, Libby. I'll take care of it. I mean, he's certainly not important enough to risk losing my job over."

"I beg your pardon," Libby said. "You're speaking of the future Mr. Libby Chessler."

"Sorry."

Libby went on to some other issues, but Sabrina didn't hear them. Her legs felt wobbly, and she leaned against the desk as she tried to absorb all that she'd just heard.

The kids at Westbridge High School wore tacky uniforms—and apparently they'd been wearing them for six months?

Libby ran the school—as dictator? Totally un-challenged by any of the other students?

Mr. Kraft was married to his secretary?

And Libby was dating Harvey and planned to marry him—as soon as she got him reinstated into high school, had his grades illegally fixed, and bought him his ticket into a prestigious college?

Sabrina gripped the edge of the secretary's desk and took several deep, calming breaths.

It's okay, she told herself. *None of this is true. It can't be true. It's just somebody's idea of a bad joke. Or some bad magic. Or . . . or a dream! Yeah, like on all those television shows. I'm going to wake up and discover it's all been a dream. Or something like that.*

Still invisible, Sabrina shook her head and stood up. *Gotta check those files.*

Carefully, slowly, she finished pulling out the S–U drawer. She flipped through the files looking for the one containing all her school records. She knew a lot of this information was on computer now, but she also knew that Mr. Kraft still didn't quite trust computers, and so he kept a paper file on everyone, as well.

Let's see . . .

Spatz, Jonathan.

Spears, Brandon.

Speering, Chelsea.

Spencer, T'kara . . .

Wait! Where's Spellman? It should be here between Speering and Spencer!

Maybe it's just out of order. She quickly flipped back through the previous files.

Then she carefully looked through every file in the Ss.

Then she checked one more time through the entire drawer.

Not there.

Don't panic! Sabrina told herself. *You exist. You're just . . . misfiled.*

"Well, that's all for tonight, Willard," Libby suddenly said. "I'm tired. Will you drive me home?"

"Certainly."

Quick! The drawer!

Libby's and Mr. Kraft's chairs screeched across the floor as they stood up and began gathering their things, and Sabrina took that opportunity to quickly close the filing cabinet drawer. Then she froze, still invisible, and watched the two turn off the lights and leave the office.

Sabrina held her breath for several minutes, and when she was certain they were gone, she immediately sat down at the secretary's desk and turned on the main school computer. In the ghostly white of the computer glow, Sabrina typed her way into the system.

"Now what are you doing?" Roland whispered as he hopped up on the desk.

But Sabrina was too intent on her quest to answer. She typed in a search requesting all records pertaining to the student Spellman, Sabrina.

Then pressed Search.

"Does this thing have any games on it?" Roland asked as they waited.

"Shhh!"

A few seconds later the computer responded.

Sabrina quickly read the words on the screen.

She couldn't breathe. Her heart seemed to stop.

Westbridge High School had absolutely no record of anyone named Spellman, Sabrina.

WOULD YOU LIKE TO TRY ANOTHER SEARCH? asked the computer.

Chapter 8

☆

"There's no place like home, there's no place like home . . ."

Like Dorothy in *The Wizard of Oz*, Sabrina felt as if she'd been tossed by a tornado into a strange, parallel world where nothing made any sense, and all she could think of was getting home.

She felt hollow and dizzy. As if she were fading away.

Her aunts would know what was going on. As full-fledged witches, they had dealt with all kinds of strange, mixed-up magic conjured by supernatural creatures from all over the Other Realm. And they'd done it for several hundred years.

All she had to do was get home to her aunts.

They'd know what to do.

Sabrina clicked the heels of her black boots together—no time to conjure up a pair of ruby slippers—then whisked herself back home.

Roland grabbed hold of her shirtsleeve just in time to be carried along with her.

They landed in a gust of wind on the front walk that led to the Spellmans' gracious old Victorian home. It sat in the snow like a vision from a Christmas card. Sabrina eagerly ran toward the front steps.

But as she stumbled onto the porch, she saw something strange. Through the white lace curtains covering the door's window she heard the sound of many voices.

Sabrina reached for the doorknob and pulled, but it seemed to be locked. She started to pop through magically when she spotted a small notice above the doorbell. DOOR LOCKED AT 10 PM. PLEASE RING FOR ADMITTANCE.

That's odd, Sabrina thought. *Sounds like a hotel.* Probably some kind of joke Salem's trying to pull.

She rang the bell and waited. And as she waited impatiently for one of her aunts to come to the door, her eyes fell upon another sign beside the door, just under the porch light:

MISS SPELLMAN'S
BOARDINGHOUSE

"Okay, now I know Salem's involved," Sabrina said to Roland. "It's probably another one of his harebrained moneymaking schemes."

She peeked in the side window and saw Salem lying on a windowsill that she knew was over a radiator. He was fatter than when she'd seen him last—a whole lot fatter. He chewed lazily at a worn mouse toy. "Ah, this is the life," she heard him sigh. "Maybe it would be just as much fun to stay a cat forever. Who cares about being human? All they do is work, work, work. Cats definitely rule." Then he fell asleep with the cat toy dangling out of his mouth.

Salem—happy to be a cat? Now, that was really weird. She tapped on the window, trying to wake him up. He opened one eye and looked at her, but he acted as if he didn't know her. He just turned over and went back to sleep.

Sabrina rang the bell again. Finally the door opened a crack, and Aunt Zelda's face poked out. But she didn't look normal. She looked tired and disheveled. And her voice didn't sound the way it usually did—warm and sophisticated and friendly. It sounded sharp and suspicious. "Yes?"

Home is where, when you go there, they have to take you in, right?

At last, here was someone who would know her and take her in. Someone who would help her make sense of what was going on tonight.

"Aunt Zelda! I'm so glad to see you!"

"Aunt?" Zelda said the word as if she had a sour taste in her mouth. "I'm nobody's aunt. What do you want?"

"Want?" Sabrina frowned in puzzlement. "I want to come in. You won't believe what's happened. I need your help—"

"I'm sorry," Zelda replied harshly. "There's no vacancy."

"Ha, ha, funny, Aunt Zelda. Who put you up to this? Salem? Are you guys in this together?"

"I don't know what you're talking about, young lady, but I said we're full up and there's no more rooms to rent." She looked Sabrina up and down. "Besides, I don't think this is your kind of place. Most of our guests are from"—she cleared her throat—"out of town."

Sabrina peered over her aunt's shoulder. The room seemed filled with all kinds of losers—supernatural losers! Trolls and fairies, witches and warlocks . . . Out of town? Out of this world, she really meant. From the Other Realm.

"Aunt Zelda!" Sabrina exclaimed. "What's going on? Where's Aunt Hilda?"

"Hilda?" Zelda spat. "Don't mention her name in this house, that useless excuse for a sister."

"What? Where is she?"

Zelda glared. "Are you some kind of friend of hers? Well, you're too late. She moved out. She's gone on tour playing electric violin for the Dave Matthews Band—a disgrace for someone with her classical musical training! I was going to tell her to never come back. But she beat me to it."

"But, Aunt Zelda—"

"Quit calling me 'Aunt'! I told you—I'm not an aunt—I don't have any nieces or nephews."

"But, Au—I mean, Miss Spellman—don't you know me? I'm Sabrina."

"I don't know any Sabrinas," Zelda said. "I never have. And I don't know your little brother there, either." She peered out into the darkness. "Tell him he needs a shave! Now, excuse me. I really don't mean to be rude, but I have no vacancies and several cranky boarders who need tending to—"

"But what about all your research? Your scientific papers?" Sabrina interrupted. "Have you given all that up for this?"

Zelda peered at Sabrina suspiciously. "How do you know about that?"

"Uh . . . I read one of your articles in a scientific journal," Sabrina fibbed. "You're very well known."

The flattery seemed to soften Zelda's manner for a moment, but then her eyes turned flat and lifeless. "Yes, well, I don't have much time for that anymore, now that Hilda's gone and left me to run this place on my own. Now, if you'll excuse me, I'll get back to work."

She didn't slam the door, but she might as well have.

Her words had slammed the door on Sabrina's heart.

If Aunt Zelda didn't know her, she would have to face the truth.

Sabrina had never been born.

☆

Chapter 9

☆

Sabrina turned around to leave and found Roland watching her from his perch on the porch railing. "Sorry, love," he said. "I warned you."

"So it's—" Sabrina's voice broke and she had to choke back a sob. "So it's true, then. I got my wish—I've never been born. I don't exist. My own father and mother wouldn't know me."

"Hey, I'm convinced," Roland replied. "That school records thing—plus Zelda . . . what more proof do you need?"

"But I don't understand!" Sabrina wailed as she leaned on the railing next to him. "I'm a no-body. I don't exist—at least not in this world. I can almost sort of understand that part. But what about Aunt Zelda and Salem and Harvey? What's wrong with them? Did somebody put some kind of spell on them, too? Why are they so different?"

Roland shook his head. "Don't you get it, Sabrina? Their lives are different because you were never born. Because you weren't there to make a difference in their lives."

"But . . . but they were all mad at me. Aunt Zelda and Aunt Hilda. And Harvey—I really got him in trouble. You'd think they'd all be happy without me around."

Roland shook his head. "Okay, it's going to get mushy here. But I'll try to keep it short and sweet." He stared up into Sabrina's eyes with the most serious look she'd ever seen on him. "Sabrina, you were an important part of their lives. Without you there, they made different choices. Their lives took different paths. Everything changed."

Sabrina ran a hand through her long blond hair. It was a pretty heavy thought. "You mean, because I wasn't there to care about Harvey, to cheer him on and be his friend, he dropped out of school and might wind up married to Libby?"

Roland nodded.

"And because I wasn't there to give them something to collaborate on, Aunt Hilda and Aunt Zelda finally got on each other's nerves enough to have a huge fight and split up?"

Roland nodded again.

"And because I'm not there, Aunt Zelda runs a boardinghouse for Other Realm losers?"

Roland frowned. "I'm not sure why that happened exactly. But yeah, that too. And since you never went to Westbridge High, Mr. Kraft never met your aunts and wound up marrying his secretary instead of falling in love with Hilda. And then Zelda. And without you to fight for the rights of the school geeks—"

"Thanks a lot!"

"—Libby completely took over the school and now rules the place like a dictator. Even Salem's life is different," Roland added. "When you lived with your aunts, you kept him from sinking into total self-absorbed laziness. You were his friend, in a weird sort of way. Now—" Roland shook his head. "He's a total mess!"

"Wow. This is really heavy to think about," Sabrina said. "You think what you do just affects yourself. You never really think much about how it affects other people's lives."

Suddenly Sabrina's eyes lit up. "What about my mom and dad? Maybe *their* lives are different, too. Maybe—without me in their lives—they never got divorced! Woo-hoo! At least *that* would be one good thing to come out of all this!"

Before Roland could say anything, Sabrina ran

back to the window where Salem lay curled up, sleeping away, and tapped on the window. "Excuse me, Salem? Salem Saberhagen?"

The black cat growled.

Sabrina used a little magic to make a can of sardines appear in her hand. She used the little key to open the can, then set it on the windowsill. Then she opened the window just a crack so the strong sardine "perfume" could waft inside and tickle Salem's sensitive nose.

One second . . . two seconds . . .

Salem sat bolt upright. "Hello? Did somebody call my name?"

"Um, you don't know me," Sabrina said quietly, so as not to draw Zelda's attention, "but I know someone you know. If you answer a question about them, I'll give you this whole can of sardines. Is it a deal?"

"Fine, sure, *anything!*" Salem said, drooling. "Zelda's got me on a diet, and I haven't had sardines in eons! In fact," he gasped, "I'm so desperate to have those sardines I'm not even wondering why I can talk to you, a mere human being, and you're not freaking out."

"Don't worry about that right now, it's complicated," Sabrina assured him. "And I promise I won't tell anyone you can talk."

"Fine, fine. Just give me the sardines!"

"Okay," Sabrina said. "But first, the question."

"Argh! What a cruel person you are, uh—what's your name?"

"Sabrina." She waited, still hoping for some glimmer of recognition in his eyes, but he simply shrugged and said, "Fine, Sabrina. Ask me your question, and I'll tell you *anything* I know!"

"Do you know Ted Spellman?" Sabrina asked.

Salem wiped the drool from his face with a little black paw. "Sure, Ted is Zelda's brother."

"Do he and his wife ever come to visit?" Sabrina asked hopefully.

"Sometimes." Salem yawned.

"His wife!" Sabrina exclaimed happily. "Oh, I *knew* it!"

"Well, *ex*-wife, I should say," Salem corrected himself. "They got divorced about seven or eight years ago." He licked his lips hungrily and gaped at the sardines. "So . . . what was your question?"

Sabrina's heart sank. "Um, no question. You already told me everything I needed to know."

"Really? Great. Glad I could help. Have a nice life. Now, *ple-e-e-ease* open this window and shove that can of sardines in here where I can reach it before I faint with desire!"

Sabrina raised the window another few inches and slid the tiny can in to Salem, who pounced on it as if he hadn't eaten in weeks.

"Bye, Salem," Sabrina whispered sadly as she closed the window again.

Slowly she walked down the steps and out onto the sidewalk. Snow had begun to fall again in soft white flakes that floated gently through the air. Sabrina barely noticed. She looked back once at her aunts' beautiful old house, then quickly looked away.

It's not home anymore, she realized. *Maybe nowhere is.*

"So, your parents got divorced anyway, huh?" Roland asked gently as he plodded along beside her in the snow.

Sabrina nodded.

"So, it wasn't your fault after all, huh?"

"What? How'd you know that's what I thought?"

Roland chuckled. "Kids always think it's their fault when their parents get a divorce. But it never is. Now you know for sure."

"Yeah, I guess. Only now I'm not even their kid, so . . . Oooh! This is too hard to think about!"

Suddenly Sabrina's head swam with the insanity of it all. And she ran—she didn't know where—just ran, hard, off into the snowy night.

Chapter 10

Sabrina found herself standing in the middle of a bridge that crossed a river in Westbridge City Park. The snow fell all around her as she stared into the icy waters below.

"Sabrina, my love! No-o-o-o-o!" Breathless from chasing after her, Roland gathered his last remaining strength, took a flying leap, and flung himself toward his favorite teenage witch.

Sabrina shrieked as he tackled her to the ground. "Roland! What are you doing?! Get off me!"

"Don't do it, Sabrina! Don't jump!" the little troll cried as he tried to pin her to the ground. "This is all my fault. I promise—I'll help you find a way out!"

Sabrina shoved him off into the snow and sat up. "Jump?" She rolled her eyes. "I wasn't going to jump. Are you crazy? I'd freeze my buns off in there! As a matter of fact, I'm well on my way to doing that right here." She jumped to her feet and brushed the snow from the back of her jeans.

"Thank goodness," Roland gasped, lying back in the snow. When his breathing slowed, he asked, "So, what were you doing?"

"Well," Sabrina said, looking out at the lights of Westbridge, "I was thinking I want to live again. I want my life back. Even with all the headaches and problems that go along with it." She helped Roland up and took him by the shoulders. "You've got to help me, Roland! Not just for me. My friends and family need me!"

"Well, I don't know," Roland replied, rubbing his hand through his beard. "The magic of the Witches' Council is pretty powerful. How about if we make a deal? You marry me, and I help you get your life back." He grinned up at her flirtatiously.

"Roland! What a miserable creep you are!" Sabrina exclaimed. Then she grinned. "Besides, you promised you'd help me fix things."

Roland took a step back. "I did? When? I don't remember—"

"Just a minute ago," Sabrina said. "When you told me it was *all your fault.* Then *promised* you'd help me find a way to fix it."

"Oh, yeah," Roland said miserably. "Well, you can't blame a guy for trying."

"So, what do we do?" Sabrina said.

"Come on," Roland replied, taking her by the hand. "I think I have an idea."

Sabrina and Roland soon stood before the Witches' Council in the Other Realm. This really did not make Sabrina feel good. She'd had a few run-ins with the Witches' Council from her very first day as a witch, when she'd messed up her first day of school so badly that she'd asked them to turn back time. She had a feeling they considered her a troublemaker and attributed it to the fact that she was part human.

"Just leave everything to me," Roland whispered. "I have an in with these guys."

"Roland, Roland, Roland," the head witch said, shaking his head.

"Y-y-yes, sir?"

"Looks like you messed up big time, little troll."

Roland blushed. "You've been watching?"

The head witch nodded gravely.

"Great," Sabrina whispered sarcastically. "You'll be a great help here."

Roland tried to explain what had happened, but the head witch just waved his hand. "Silence. We've seen enough. And we're much too busy to deal with this little problem—"

"Hey, I resent that crack!" the little troll said, pulling himself up to his full height.

"Me, too!" Sabrina agreed. "Me not being born isn't a little problem. At least, not to me."

The head witch pounded his gavel. "Order in the court!"

Sabrina and Roland zipped their lips and crossed their fingers.

"Now," the head witch continued, "we on the Witches' Council do not take lightly wishes to be unborn. First of all, we think it's a very ungrateful attitude, and in the second place, it's very complicated magic to accomplish. So we have decided to turn your case over to the 'You Bet Your Life!' subcommittee. They will hear your case and decide what to do."

"But, sir—" Sabrina and Roland said at once.

Bang! The gavel hit the desk again. "You're dismissed. Next order of business . . ."

A bailiff came and escorted them from the Witches' Council chambers. He led them down a long and twisting hallway. At last they stopped before another door.

"Why is there a sandwich painted on this door?" Roland asked the bailiff.

"Well, duh!" the guy replied and opened the door.

Sabrina groaned. "Oh, I get it. The *sub* committee. *Sub* sandwich?"

"Sub sandwich?" Roland asked. "Is that anything like a hoagie?"

Sabrina nodded. "Submarine sandwich. Hoagie. Grinder. Hero."

The subcommittee chairman was just popping the last bite of his sandwich into his mouth. He licked his fingers and grinned. "Delicious," he said, then looked up at Sabrina, Roland, and the bailiff.

"Well, well, well, now, who do we have here?"

Sabrina noticed that the man looked a lot like Groucho Marx. He had huge black eyebrows, which he kept wiggling up and down, and a huge black mustache that looked painted on.

The bailiff told Sabrina to stand over by the microphone, then he handed the chairman her case folder.

The chairman quickly flipped through the pages, then promptly tossed the whole thing over his shoulder. The papers fell from the folder and scattered all over the floor. "Well, whaddaya know. This girl's never been born. So I guess we don't have a case." He banged his gavel on his desk and shouted, "Bailiff! Send out for more subs!"

"Wait!" Sabrina cried. "This is serious."

"Serious?" the chairman said seriously. "Why, I've never heard anything so ridiculous in all my life. How come I see you if you've never been born?" He burped. "Maybe it was something I ate. Bailiff!" he shouted. "Leave the hot peppers off the next sandwich. It's giving me nightmares."

"I am not a nightmare!" Sabrina exclaimed. "I'm a girl. A teenage witch. I just have to undo my wish that I had never been born. It was just all a big mistake."

"Well, well, well, Miss Spellman, let's not get huffy." He sat back in his chair and thought a minute. "I'll tell you what I'm going to do. I'll give you a chance to double your money—whaddaya think, folks?"

He turned toward the rest of the room, and Sabrina followed his gaze.

"Hey!" She realized now that the room was full of people who had come to listen to the hearing. Only they were acting like the audience at a game show, clapping and cheering and shouting things at the subcommittee chairman.

Okay, Sabrina thought. *This mania for game shows is really getting out of hand. . . .*

"This is ridiculous," she whispered to Roland.

"Hey, go with the flow," Roland whispered back. "You might get your life back. And maybe even earn back some of the missing charity money, too."

"I never thought of that." She turned toward the chairman. "Okay, I'll go for it."

The audience applauded.

"I think we've got a live one here, folks!" the chairman joked in an aside to the audience. "Okay, now," he said to Sabrina, "for five hundred dollars—answer this question in thirty seconds or less."

Sabrina clutched hands with Roland, nervously awaiting her question. "And if I can't answer?" she asked.

The guy shrugged. "Then 'You Bet Your Life!' "

The audience burst into applause again.

"This is ridiculous," Sabrina muttered.

"What did you say, miss?" the chairman demanded.

"Oh, uh, I said this is exciting!" Sabrina replied with a great big smile. "What's my question?"

The chairman reached toward a huge deck of cards on his desk. He made a grand show of removing the top one. Then he flipped it over and read it.

Ding, ding, ding! A bell rang, and confetti fell down from the sky. "Whaddaya know," said the chairman, "it's a Quest Card."

Uh-oh. Sabrina didn't like the sound of that. "What's a Quest Card?"

"It means I have to send you on a quest," the chairman replied. "Something you must accomplish in order to get your life back."

"Oh, you mean like a treasure hunt?" Roland guessed.

"Not exactly," said the chairman. "More like a test."

"Uh-oh," Roland muttered. "I don't like the sound of this."

People called out ideas from the audience.

"No, too easy," the chairman said. Or "too boring." Or "totally illegal."

The room was getting noisy as people talked and laughed and called out suggestions. Nothing seemed to suit the chairman.

Sabrina grew more and more upset. *They're acting like this is a real game show, and not my life.*

"So what do I have to do to get my life back?" she finally exclaimed impatiently. "Build a pyramid? Get a taxi in New York City during rush hour? Create world peace?"

Silence filled the room. Then . . .

"GOOD SUGGESTION!" the chairman shouted.

Bells rang! The audience burst into wild cheers!

Sabrina groaned.

"You've got twenty-four hours," the chairman said without a trace of a smile. Then he turned toward the audience and wiggled his eyebrows up and down. "Let's hear it for our contestant, Miss Sabrina Spellman!"

The audience cheered as the chairman pushed a button. Then—"Eeeeek!"—a trapdoor opened beneath Sabrina and Roland's feet and they fell out of the room.

Minutes later Sabrina landed on her behind in the snow. She looked around. "We're back in Westbridge," she said.

And then it hit her.

She had twenty-four hours to achieve world peace.

Oh, heavens! Would she be able to get her life back?

Would she be able to accomplish the impossible?

Chapter 11

☆

☆

"It's hopeless, Roland. There's absolutely no way." She and Roland sat in the park trying to figure out what to do.

"Maybe not," Roland said hopefully.

"Oh, give me a break. The world's a mess. Crime, war, poverty. How's one young witch supposed to fix things—all by herself?"

Roland shrugged. "Maybe it's a trick question."

Sabrina's eyes lit up. "Roland, maybe you're right. Maybe I can just use my magic." She closed her eyes and tried to remember some spell that would work. *Oh, if only I had my* Discovery of Magic *book!*

"Maybe I can make up something." She closed her eyes and thought hard.

Peace on earth, goodwill toward people,
Make it more than a holiday song,
End the wars and all the fighting,
So that all the world's people can get
*   along.*

Sabrina waved her arms in the air, then opened her eyes and looked around.

Nothing happened.

But early morning sun made the snowy world sparkle like a Christmas card. The world seemed like a beautiful, peaceful place.

"Seems pretty peaceful to me," Roland said, looking around. "Maybe it worked!"

"Do you really think so?" Sabrina asked.

As they watched, they saw two young boys walking into the park. They laughed happily as they skipped and played.

A very peaceful scene.

Then one of the boys tripped and fell on his face in the dirt. After a second he jumped and pushed the other boy. "You tripped me!" they heard him yell.

"I did not," the other boy shouted right back.

"Did, too."

"Did not!"

Soon both boys were tumbling on the ground, punching each other like cowboys.

Out on the street a horn blared, and its driver

rolled down his window and shouted something rude at another car.

A gray-haired man walked by reading a newspaper with the headline "Fighting Erupts in Middle East."

A teenager bopped by and tossed his soda can on the ground just two feet away from the trashcan.

"Okay. Looks like *that* didn't work!" Sabrina said. "I guess world peace is not one of those things a witch can achieve with a zap and a rhyme."

"Maybe you just need to start with the little things?" Roland suggested, wiggling his eyebrows up and down. "Like me? I don't care whether you exist or not," he said. "I'll marry you anyway."

"Oh, Roland, you've been very kind to me these last few hours, but I'm really not ready to get married—to anyone. I'm too young."

But maybe, she thought, *he's got a good idea.*

Maybe she should start with the little things. *Maybe I don't know how to achieve world peace,* she thought. *Maybe I can't fix all the problems in the world. But maybe I could start with little things. Maybe I can do something to fix the problems of the people I love. Maybe I can bring a little bit of peace to Harvey's world. And my aunts' world. And Salem's . . .*

"Okay," she said. "What have I got to lose?"

Just my life, said a little voice in her head.

* * *

Sabrina raced home.

The first thing she did when she got there was zap up a huge family message center and put it on the wall next to the fridge. It had a dry erase marker board, a place for a calendar, a bulletin board for posting notes, and a pad of those little pink "While You Were Out" message notes. No way would any messages get lost if everybody used this.

Okay, so maybe I'll never get back here and be able to use it. But it's a start.

Next Sabrina found her favorite picture of her aunts as young women. They were wearing long party dresses and they were smiling and had their arms around each other, the best of friends.

With a quick snap of her fingers, Sabrina made two copies of the photo, then zapped up two envelopes.

To Zelda she wrote, Someone loves you and misses you and wants to come home.

To Hilda she wrote, Someone loves you and misses you and wants you to come home.

She slipped a picture in with each note, then posted Zelda's on the bulletin board and popped Hilda's into the toaster.

Next she blinked up a small smoke alarm. Using her magic, she converted it into a "Bicker Meter" and placed it on the ceiling above the breakfast table. Once Hilda came back—if she ever did—the Bicker Meter would go off whenever their squabbles got out of hand. She hoped that would remind them to "put out the fire."

Was there anything else she could do here?

Salem.

There he was, still lying on the windowsill over the radiator, the empty sardine can on the floor. What could she do to snap Salem out of his stupor?

Sabrina snapped her fingers, and a young girl cat appeared in the entry way. "Meow?" she said sweetly.

Salem's eyes popped open. "Well, hello there, Miss Kitty!" He leaped down to join her.

Sabrina laughed. *That'll jerk a knot in his chain!* She knew that within the half hour, he'd be telling the new cat about his latest schemes to make a million dollars and take over the world.

Next Sabrina looked up the address of Sam's Garage and zapped herself over to check up on Harvey. She found him under the hood of a car, working on the motor. His clothes were streaked with grease, and he didn't seem to have his heart in his work.

"*Kinkle!*" Sam the boss hollered. "That work was supposed to be done an hour ago! Get a move on!"

Harvey pulled his head out from under the hood. Sabrina could tell by the scowl on his face that he was about to shout something ugly back, which would only make his boss yell at him even more. Which would make Harvey feel even less like doing a good job.

And people wonder how wars get started.

Before Harvey could utter a word, Sabrina quickly cast a spell over boss and employee:

> *When you're mad at a dude*
> *and want to yell at the guy,*
> *Tell him what's wrong*
> *And explain to him why.*

Okay, so the greeting card poetry was a little corny, Sabrina admitted to herself, but she didn't care as long as it did the trick.

For a moment Harvey looked as if he'd lost his voice. He coughed and cleared his throat, then said, "I'm trying my best, boss. But I could really use some help. You really know an awful lot about cars. Could you help me figure this out?"

Sam's mouth fell open in shock.

For a moment, Sabrina worried that maybe her spell was a little off. What if Sam thought Harvey was being a smart aleck?

Then Sam's scowl dissolved. "Well, sure, son," he replied. "What seems to be the problem?"

He joined Harvey under the hood, and soon they were discussing the problem as if they were father and son. She even saw Sam pat Harvey on the back!

Just then the phone rang. Sam went over and answered politely, "Hello, Sam's Garage. How may I help you?" He listened for a moment, and then said, "No, you don't have the wrong number. This is Sam. What's up, honey? . . . I know I'm late, and I apologize. But I was helping my young employee Harvey figure out the problem with this carburetor. He's a good kid, knows a lot about cars. . . . I know, I know. How about this, sweetheart? How about if I pick up some Chinese and bring Harvey home so you can meet him? . . . That's fine, dear. Now, you go take a bubble bath and we'll be home in about forty-five minutes. Love you! Bye-bye."

Sabrina had to smother her laughter to see big old grungy Sam talking so sweetly to his wife.

It's working, she thought. *It's a trickle, but it's working.*

When Harvey was nice to Sam, it made Sam feel better, so he was nice to his wife. His wife, after soaking in a bubble bath, would probably be a cheerful hostess when Harvey came over. A chain reaction. Just going in a better direction.

"Kind of like a chain letter, huh?" Roland whispered.

Sabrina nodded.

Roland sighed. "I broke one of those once."

"What happened?" Sabrina asked him.

"Well, I used to be six foot three instead of three foot six."

Sabrina zapped them over to the coffee shop to see what she could do to help out there. A long line had formed as Josh hurried to fix multiple complex coffee orders.

"Do you have any tea?" Sabrina asked above all the noise.

"Tea?" someone said.

Josh looked at her without recognizing her, of course. "Yeah, we've got all kinds of tea. What would you like?"

"A cup of green tea would be nice. How about you, Roland?"

"Maybe some Earl Grey?"

Josh soon held out two steaming cups as people in the crowd discussed Sabrina's bold selection.

"You know, this place is really nice," she told Josh.

"Thanks."

"But you know what would be *really* nice?"

Josh frowned. "What?"

"Some soft music. Like some classical. Or smooth jazz. You ought to try it."

Josh shrugged. "Sure, why not."

He turned on the soft jazz channel on the radio. Mellow wordless music flowed out into the room.

And then Sabrina realized a lot of people were

carrying small pots of tea to their tables instead of high-octane espressos.

And slowly, gradually, the mood of the room began to change. Everyone seemed to relax. A few people struck up conversations with people they didn't know. A couple of people began to read.

Sabrina sipped her green tea and smiled.

But then the door slammed open. Willard Kraft burst into the room. "I need a double espresso—pronto!" he ordered, striding up to the counter. "It's an emergency. I'm dead on my feet and I've got a party to get to in fifteen minutes!"

"Shhhhhhh!" said a couple of people around the room.

Mr. Kraft looked around. "What's going on here? Some kind of cult thing?"

"Everyone's just relaxing," Sabrina spoke up. "Maybe you should try it. Would you"—and she couldn't believe she was saying this—"care to join me? The tea here is excellent."

"Tea? Well, okay." Mr. Kraft looked at the tea menu. "I'll try a cup of Irish breakfast tea with sugar and a twist of lemon."

A few moments later he dumped his coat in the extra chair and sat down with Sabrina. "I don't think I know you. Do you go to Westbridge High?" he asked.

Sabrina wasn't sure what to answer at first. But then she realized the truth was, for now, "No."

"How about your little brother?" Mr. Kraft asked. "Do you go to Westbridge Elementary?"

Roland started to growl back a retort, but Sabrina pinched him under the table and said, "He goes to . . . private school. For the gifted."

Roland seemed to like that, and he sipped his tea without another remark.

Mr. Kraft took a long sip of his tea. "Mmm. Why . . . that's delicious." He sat back in his chair and relaxed. But then a tear filled his eye.

"Are you all right?" Sabrina asked, suddenly worried. She'd never seen him cry.

Mr. Kraft waved his hand in the air. "It's nothing, really. It's just that . . . my Irish grandmother used to fix Irish breakfast tea for me when I was a little boy. And these homemade scones . . . I'd forgotten all about it till now. The taste and aroma of this tea just brings it all back. It's as if she's here with me somehow."

Wow, Sabrina thought. *That* is *good tea!* She handed him a paper napkin and he dabbed at his eyes. For the next twenty minutes Willard Kraft turned into a different kind of guy as he told Sabrina tales of his grandmother from Ireland.

But she knew she had more things to do, so she got up to leave and introduced Mr. Kraft to the gentleman at the next table. She left them chatting about their respective grandmothers.

For the next few hours Sabrina wandered around town, looking for little things to do.

She helped a cross-looking old lady cross the street. Then she watched the old lady help a young girl in a wheelchair get through the door of a store.

Sabrina picked up some litter and tossed it in a trashcan.

A kid hanging out by himself was just about to throw his soda can on the ground. When he saw her, he thought twice and instead tossed it like a basketball into the trash.

"Wow!" Roland said. "I bet he's great at the free-throw line!"

A couple of kids heading toward the park with a basketball saw it, too, and asked the boy to join them in a game.

She walked by Libby Chessler's house and . . .

Never mind, she thought, walking on by. *After all, I've only got twenty-four hours!*

Soon her time was almost up.

She tried to think of some grand schemes to try to reach more people.

"What if I did something to block out all the news programs, so people all over the world couldn't see—and copy—the horrible things on the news?" But then she shook her head. Keeping people from knowing the truth wouldn't make it stop happening. People had been fighting long before television and radio news.

So she just kept doing little things, hoping that every time she made a difference in someone else's life—even if it was a little thing—they in turn would do something positive in someone else's life.

The cool vibes might just make it all the way around the world . . . in a couple hundred years.

At last her time ran out.

"It's time to go," Roland told her.

"Yeah," Sabrina sighed. She hadn't achieved world peace, but she'd done a few good deeds. And she felt pretty cool about that.

When they arrived at the "You Bet Your Life!" subcommittee, Sabrina was nervous. So nervous she couldn't even eat her sub sandwich.

The chairman banged his gavel on his desk. Then he asked Sabrina to step forward.

"Let's welcome back yesterday's contestant, Miss Sabrina Spellman!"

The audience clapped and cheered. Sabrina had the feeling they'd clap and cheer no matter what the chairman said.

"So, Miss Spellman," he said. "How did you do with your quest?"

Sabrina cleared her throat and looked around. What should she say? She'd come nowhere near close to making a dent in the world peace issue. But she felt okay about the things she had done. One by one she told what she had done. The chairman let her speak without interruption. The audience didn't make a sound.

"Well," Sabrina said at last. "That's about it. I couldn't figure out how to create world peace. So I just tried to do as much as I could little by little. . . ."

When no one said anything, Sabrina ended with, "That's it."

The audience held its breath.

The chairman peered at her, tapping his fingers thoughtfully on his desk.

And as she waited, Sabrina realized something important. She'd probably totally lost this silly game. She surely hadn't won her life back.

But she remembered something her father had told her one night as they ate Chinese takeout, something an ancient Chinese scholar had written, and she found herself saying it aloud: "It is better to light one candle than to curse the darkness."

"Whoa!" Roland whispered. "That's heavy!"

The chairman nodded, deep in thought. Then he wiggled his eyebrows, mugged for the audience, and quipped, "That's all well and good, miss, but what's that got to do with whirled peas?"

"Huh?" Sabrina and Roland looked at one another.

"What are you talking about?" Sabrina asked.

The chairman laughed. "Haven't you seen all

those bumper stickers around Westbridge that say 'Visualize world peace'? Well I saw another one recently that was kind of a spoof of that. It said 'Visualize whirled peas.' " He grinned at her.

"But—but that's a meaningless joke!" Sabrina sputtered.

The chairman nodded, and he looked Sabrina straight in the eye. "Some people think life is a meaningless joke."

Sabrina gulped. "Did I say that?" She thought back to her pre-wish evening. "Yeah, I guess I did. But I didn't really mean that. And now more than ever, I want my life back," she said. "Even when it's miserable, it's wonderful."

The chairman smiled a half-smile.

"Um, I'd like to call a five-minute recess," Roland asked. "Ten minutes, max."

"Fine," the chairman said. He banged his gavel. "Bailiff, call out for more sub sandwiches! And tell them to use a little more oil and vinegar this time!"

"More subs!" the bailiff called out.

Meanwhile, Roland grabbed Sabrina by the arm and pulled her out into the hallway. "Sabrina, you know that bumper stick that reads 'Question authority'?"

"Yeah, I've seen that one," Sabrina said.

"Okay, well, don't do that right now. This is all pretty nutty, but we might pull out of this crash and burn alive. So don't question the chairman's authority or logic. Just do what he says, okay?"

"Okay."

Roland held out his hand. "Go ahead. Zap me up a bowlful of mushy green peas."

This is so silly, Sabrina thought. But under the circumstances, she didn't have much choice. "Okay." She raised her hand in the air and chanted this spell:

Of all the vegetables laid on my plate,
My favorite are little green peas.
Make me a bowl of this delicate treat,
And mush 'em up good, pretty please.

They were back in the subcommittee room in four and a half. Sabrina held up a bowl of fluffy green whirled peas.

The chairman took them from her and took a dramatic sniff. He wiggled his eyebrows, and a smile played across his lips. Then he slipped out his dentures, left them chattering on the desktop, scooped up a spoonful of whirled peas, and took a bite. "Mmmm, perfect! Like fresh from the garden, only . . . mushier!"

Sabrina and Roland stood silently and watched the chairman eat the entire bowlful. Then he wiped his mouth on his tie, popped his dentures back in, and sat back in his chair. "Hey, we knew there was no way in the world one teenage witch could achieve world peace in twenty-four hours. Come on—we were only kidding ya! It's impossible! Our powers just don't work that way. But hey, frankly, we're pretty darn impressed with how you tackled the job anyway." He wiggled his brows up and down. "Wanna go for a bonus question?"

"No, thanks!" Sabrina said firmly but politely. "I just want to get home!"

"Okay." He shrugged. "Well, you've been a lot of laughs today, Miss Spellman. Hasn't she, audience?"

The audience clapped and cheered. Somebody whistled.

"So, Dennis," the chairman went on, "tell our lovely contestant what she's won today."

Brisk game show music began to play as colored lights flashed around the subcommittee room.

"You've won the deluxe edition of the 'You Bet Your Life!' home game, a year's supply of Turtle Wax, a $2 off coupon at your local sub shop, and . . . your life back!"

"Congratulations!" the chairman exclaimed. "And thanks for playing 'You Bet Your Life!' See you next time!"

The audience applauded. The chairman waved. Roland gave her knee a congratulatory hug.

And then suddenly Sabrina began to spin.

Round and round, faster and faster, she felt as if she were spinning within Dorothy's tornado in *The Wizard of Oz,* her hair flying out around her, and then—BUMP!

She was home again. In her aunt's old Victorian house.

She looked around the front entryway. Were things back to normal? There was only one way to find out.

She pounded up the old wooden stairs to the second floor. She flung open the door to her own bedroom—

"Yes!" It was filled with all her own things! She ran around the room, throwing open her closet, pulling open her drawers. Her lava lamp was bubbling. There were dirty socks under the bed. A picture of her mom and dad sat on the nightstand.

And Salem looked up from his spot on the windowsill.

"Where ya been and what did ya bring me?" Salem purred.

Sabrina scooped up the surprised cat and danced him around the room.

"Dorothy was right!" she told him. "There's no place like home. There's no place like home!"

Chapter 12

☆

☆

"I *love* this new family message center!" Aunt Zelda exclaimed. She looked through her reading glasses and wrote a neat note about an upcoming meeting of the Independent Scientists Society on the new calendar.

They were home earlier than expected from the Time Warp Clock Convention. Apparently someone had made a mistake on the program about when it actually ended.

The coolest thing about Sabrina's entire adventure with the "You Bet Your Life!" subcommittee?

They had returned her home to Friday night, just a few minutes later than when Roland had granted her wish.

"I think it's great, too," Hilda said. "But it's almost Christmas. How come you're giving this to us now?"

"I couldn't wait," Sabrina said. "And I wanted to give it to you guys as a way to apologize for the missing message from the Other Realm."

"Oh, don't worry about that," Zelda told her. "The meeting wasn't all that important anyway. It was just Drell throwing his weight around again, trying to look important."

"Now, as for this Bicker Meter—I'm not sure about that," Hilda said. "I don't think we really need that."

"Well, I think it's wonderful," Aunt Zelda said.

"You would," Hilda replied. "You'll probably use it to blame me for all our squabbles."

"I will not, Hilda Spellman! Now, you take that back!"

"I will not," Hilda said. "You're always trying to—"

BING! BING! BING! BING! BING!

Zelda and Hilda looked overhead at the Bicker Meter. Then they both laughed.

"Maybe we do need it after all," Hilda admitted.

"Let's see how long we can go without setting it off," Zelda suggested. "We'll make a game of it."

Suddenly Hilda stood up. "Come on, Zelda. I don't know why, but I've got this funny feeling— like I want to go look at our old photo albums."

Giggling like young sisters, Sabrina's two aunts hurried up the stairs.

Just then the doorbell rang. Sabrina answered the door.

"Harvey!"

He stood there covered in snowflakes, without saying a word. And Sabrina thought he looked absolutely *wonderful*—like his old self again.

But he still wasn't saying anything, he was just twisting his gloves in his hand.

Was he still mad at her? Was he going to yell at her again about the money?

I don't care! Sabrina thought happily. *I'm just glad to have him back in my life any way I can.*

"Listen, Harvey, I'm really—"

"Sabrina, listen, I'm really—"

"Sorry," they both said at the same time.

Sabrina was surprised. *"You're* sorry?"

"Yeah." He dug his toe in the snow that had drifted up on the wooden porch. "I never should have gotten mad at you like that about the money. I feel terrible about it. You didn't deserve to get yelled at."

"But, Harvey," Sabrina said, "I lost all that money—"

"I know! But that's not the point. You see, I get really nervous around money—I don't know why. And on top of everything, what I didn't tell you was that the coach yelled at me at basketball practice for fouling up all my foul shots. So I was feeling kind of like a loser to begin with."

"Oh, Harvey, I'm sorry."

"It was like a chain reaction," he went on. "The coach yelled at me. Then I yelled at you. I bet I ruined your evening, too."

"Well," Sabrina said, "let's just say I was sad we weren't talking."

Harvey reached out and took her hand. "Anybody can make a mistake," he said miserably. "But nobody can cheer me up like you."

Sabrina felt tears well up in her eyes. She threw her arms around him and hugged him tight. "Oh, thank you, Harvey. You don't know how good it feels to hear you say that!"

When she let go of him, he was blushing, but he had that cheerful lopsided grin on his face, the look that was so Harvey. "Does this mean you forgive me?"

Sabrina laughed. "We'll forgive each other."

"So, listen." Harvey pulled a jar filled with bills and coins out of his coat pocket. "I brought over all the cash I could scrape up so we could sort of, you know, pool all our resources. See how much we've got. Maybe we can take out a loan at the bank!" he joked. "Anyway, I'm sure we can figure out some way to come up with the money . . . together."

Sabrina felt as if her smile might outshine the

porch light. "Sure we can. I mean, the kids at the children's home are counting on us. We can't let them down on Christmas—"

"Boo-hoo-hoo! *Stop it!* You're breaking my heart!" someone said just inside the front door.

Sabrina and Harvey turned around.

"Who's that?" Harvey said.

Sabrina opened the front door, but all they saw was a black cat sitting on the rug pawing at his eyes as if he were crying.

"Salem!" Sabrina quickly scooped the bawling cat up into her arms. "Shhh! Shhh! There now," she whispered, hoping Salem would get the hint and quit talking. "Um, I think that was the television, Harvey. Wait here. I'll just go turn it off." She hurried into the kitchen with Salem in her arms.

"Salem! What's going on? You almost let Harvey hear you talk!"

But Salem was still crying too hard to worry about it. "I confess!" he sobbed. "I have the money."

"What money?" Sabrina said, and then her eyes popped open wide. "You mean our club money?"

Salem nodded his head.

Sabrina sat the cat down on the counter and folded her arms. "Okay, buster. Explain."

"Oka-a-ay," he said, still sniffling. "But could I have a tissue first, please?"

Sabrina snapped a tissue into her hand, then

helped Salem dry his eyes. "Okay, now. Go ahead."

"Well," Salem began, "it all started when I ran out on the porch to see if it had stopped snowing. I found some money in a plain envelope that had fallen into the bushes right beside the front steps—as if it had been delivered right to me by the paper boy."

"My money!" Sabrina gasped. "You mean I dropped it right in front of the house?"

Salem nodded. "I thought my wishes had come true! Money falling out of the sky! There was no name on the envelope, no way to trace who'd lost it. So I . . . I kept it." He buried his face beneath his paws. "I'm so ashamed!"

"Well, where is it?" Sabrina asked him, then gasped. "You didn't spend it, did you?"

"No!" Salem replied, standing up now and flicking his long black tail. "Not one thin dime. I guess I knew deep down that it belonged to somebody and that I was going to have to mention it to you or your aunts so we could find the owner. But I just needed a little time . . . to make myself part with all that Christmas gre-e-e-nery." Salem dissolved into sobs again.

"Now, now, don't start up again," Sabrina told him. And then suddenly she gave him a nice warm hug. It was so nice to have the old scheming Salem Saberhagen back. Obnoxious was better than wimpy.

"Uh, what was *that* for?" Salem asked.

"Oh, just because," Sabrina said with a grin. "Now, tell me where the money is."

"I've been sitting on it. *Literally.*" He leaped off the kitchen counter and trotted over to a cat bed in the corner of the kitchen. Sabrina lifted up the pillow and saw an envelope underneath. "Harvey!" she exclaimed. "Come here! Quick!"

Harvey rushed into the kitchen. "Sabrina! What's wrong?"

"Nothing's wrong," Sabrina crowed as she held up the white envelope. "I found our money. Look!"

Together they quickly counted it.

"It's all here," Harvey said. "Every single dime."

"What did I tell you?" Salem mouthed silently from behind Harvey's back.

Harvey laughed out loud. "This is great. But I can't believe your *cat* had it! That's a story for the newspapers."

"No!" Sabrina exclaimed. "I mean, uh, Salem's shy. He really doesn't like to have his picture taken."

Harvey shrugged. "Well, anyway, we've got the money back. So everything's fine. Want to go shopping for the Christmas party in the morning with me?"

"Definitely," Sabrina said.

"So, what do you want to do now?" Harvey asked with a twinkle in his eye.

Sabrina slipped her hand into his. "I think I'd love to take a long walk in the snow with the nicest boy I know."

"Cool." Harvey smiled. Then frowned. "Um, does that mean with me?"

"You bet!"

Together they turned up their collars and walked out into the night. The snow falling on Westbridge made the whole world seem like a magical snow dome.

Merry Christmas, Westbridge, Sabrina thought happily. *Merry Christmas, World!*

"Hey, there's a good movie on later," Harvey told her. "Want to go over to my house and watch it?"

"Sure," Sabrina replied. "What's the name of it?"

"It's a Wonderful Life. Did you ever see it?"

See it? Sabrina thought with a grin. *I* lived *it!*

But all she said was, "Yeah, I've seen it. In fact, it's one of my favorite movies of all time."

"Really?" Harvey said. "Mine, too. Isn't that wonderful?"

"Yeah," Sabrina agreed.

About the Author

Cathy East Dubowski loves the Christmas movie *It's a Wonderful Life* and watches her own copy of the video at least once every year during the holidays. That story was the inspiration for *It's a Miserable Life!*

Cathy has written many books for kids, including *Sabrina, the Teenage Witch* titles *Santa's Little Helper, A Dog's Life,* and *Fortune Cookie Fox,* as well as *Salem's Tails* books *Salem Goes to Rome* and *Psychic Kitty.* She's also written for *The Secret World of Alex Mack, The Mystery Files of Shelby Woo,* and *The Journey of Allen Strange.*

One of Cathy's original books for young readers, *Cave Boy,* illustrated by husband Mark Dubowski, was chosen as an International Reading Association/CBC Children's Choice.

Cathy writes on an iMac in an old red barn in the backyard of her home in North Carolina, where she lives with Mark, daughters Lauren and Megan, and their two golden retrievers, Macdougal and Morgan.